"I'm pretty much a lost cause in the roma

Christa was abo
because that wa
ever heard, and
last few years…

But then Tug went on.

"We lost her mom three years ago."

A widower. Raising kids alone. The revelation sparked her sympathy. "I'm so sorry."

He acknowledged her words with a look of appreciation. "Thank you. I won't pretend it's been easy," he added frankly as they neared her door, "but we're doing all right on our own. Just like we are. And while I hate to disappoint my resident matchmaker, that's how it's going to stay. I've got enough on my plate. As you can plainly see."

They'd reached her classroom.

She paused.

So did he.

And when she looked up and met his gaze, she read the sorrow and sincerity there, and that expression—that singular look—was enough to make her wish he'd give romance a second chance.

Multipublished bestselling author
Ruth Logan Herne loves God, her country,
her family, dogs, chocolate and coffee! Married
to a very patient man, she lives in an old
farmhouse in Upstate New York and thinks
possums should leave the cat food alone and
snakes should always live outside. There are
no exceptions to either rule! Visit Ruth at
ruthloganherne.com.

Learning to Trust

Ruth Logan Herne

LOVE INSPIRED
INSPIRATIONAL ROMANCE

LOVE INSPIRED®
INSPIRATIONAL ROMANCE

ISBN-13: 978-1-335-48809-1

Learning to Trust

For questions and comments about the quality of this book,
please contact us at CustomerService@Harlequin.com.

Love Inspired
22 Adelaide St. West, 40th Floor
Toronto, Ontario M5H 4E3, Canada
www.Harlequin.com

Printed in U.S.A.

And these words, which I command thee this day, shall be in thine heart: And thou shalt teach them diligently unto thy children, and shalt talk of them when thou sittest in thine house, and when thou walkest by the way, and when thou liest down, and when thou risest up.
—*Deuteronomy* 6:6–7

This one is for Lisa, a wonderful and masterful elementary school teacher who makes things come alive for kids with special needs and everyone she comes in contact with...
She is a great mom, great daughter, great sister, great wife and a dear friend.
The kind I can make fun of and laugh with and, yes, occasionally cry with.
To Lisa...with love. You brat.

Chapter One

The elementary-school principal wanted a meeting ASAP regarding Tug Moyer's overachieving daughter. Tug's boss had requested a similar face-to-face conference because he'd broken protocol to save two little boys from a hostage situation an hour before and the Central Washington deputy sheriff hadn't eaten since last night.

Must be Monday.

The good news was the preschool boys were being checked out at the local hospital, where they were met by a woman from child services. They were alive. They'd suffered no physical harm and maybe they were young enough to escape with no emotional trauma.

He explained to the soon-to-retire sheriff that he had to stop at the school, pulled into the parking lot of Golden Grove Elementary two minutes later and walked in the front door.

"Tug Moyer." Ivy Harrington beamed at him from her chair behind the reception desk inside the door. The seventy-two-year-old woman wasn't meant to guard anything, but she could push the alarm button that issued a silent 911 call and/or the door-opening button, and she'd only confused the two a few times.

Minor details for a woman who'd taught Golden Grove kids for over forty years.

"Miss Ivy, how are you?" He motioned to the check-in roster. "I'm on my way to Evangeline's class. Can you write me in?"

"That's not protocol," she scolded, but grinned. "But for you, I'll do it."

"I appreciate it." He flashed her a smile, then turned.

Three people stood forty feet ahead of him. Three very unhappy people, including Evangeline.

He wiped the grin off his face, but not before they saw it. The principal and the younger woman frowned in tandem. Then the principal tapped her watch. "You've kept all of us waiting, Terrence."

Uh-oh. His given name. He'd been named Terrence Michael nearly four decades back, but he'd been called Tug for as long as he could recall. "I'm sorry, Mrs. Menendez. I was in a bit of a situation when the original text came in. Hazard of the job." He turned toward the other woman and tried not to notice how pretty she was, but he'd have to be dead or blind and he was neither.

Her dark hair was pulled back from an oval face. Sculpted brows arched over smoky eyes, eyes that were neither gray nor brown, but a blend of both. He reached out a hand in greeting and tried not to notice she wasn't wearing anyone's ring because he never noticed things like that.

He did now. "Ms. Alero, I presume? We haven't had the pleasure of meeting yet. I'm Deputy Moyer. Evangeline's father."

"I know who you are." The teacher gave him one of those classic elementary-schoolteacher looks. Hard. Firm. Unyielding. He'd gotten his share of those back in the day but hadn't been privy to one in a long time. The attractive teacher brought that winning streak to an end. "At this point," she continued, "I'm pretty sure half the world knows who you are."

The exaggeration made him frown. As a deputy, he'd been doing online self-help videos for kids for several years. *The Fire Within* was a totally volunteer Christian cop kind of thing, and every now and again one of his posts went viral. In the internet age, that was a good thing.

"The online world has a new hero, it seems." She folded her arms lightly. "Or in this case, heroine."

He looked from woman to woman. "I'm confused. Did my video from last night offend someone? Because I'm not sure how urging kids to seek help in times of stress can be a bad thing."

The principal hummed, then aimed a look down at Evangeline.

The teacher followed.

And his absolutely beautiful, precocious daughter squirmed. He squatted down and got face-to-face with the guilty-looking girl. "Vangie, what did you do?"

"Exactly what you showed me to do."

The teacher made a sound of disapproval.

Tug ignored it.

He kept his focus on Evangeline. "I don't know what you're talking about."

"Making videos. You know. We do that all the time."

They did. Both kids saw him making videos for his

social-media page. With Nathan, six, and Vangie, nearly nine, he'd recently started showing them how to shoot a video of themselves that they could send to various family members. "You made a video?"

"Dad." She clasped his hands in hers. Her voice held appeal, and when Vangie embraced her I-know-best persona, Tug knew he was in for a serious reckoning. Despite her age, Evangeline Moyer was pretty sure she should be ruler of the universe and was always surprised when the world disagreed.

"What on earth did you do, child?"

"You really don't know?" The teacher's voice smacked of doubt. "When something goes viral on social media, your phone must be sending you alerts. Haven't your friends and family been texting you?"

His phone.

He'd silenced it because he'd been knee-deep in a life-and-death situation on Old Orchard Road.

He pulled his phone out of his pocket as he answered her. "Ma'am, I do a daily encouragement video blog for teens, and every now and again one of my posts hits it big." He lifted his shoulders in a frank shrug. "While that's complimentary, the most important thing is reaching the one kid that really needs those words that day. It's not about how many shares or Tweets or—"

He stopped as his gaze dropped to his phone.

He stared.

Two million views already, and the popular post had gone live seven hours ago.

Seven hours...

He'd posted his video to go live at midnight. That was fourteen hours ago. That meant he was on his way

to work when this one hit the internet. Vangie and Nathan were catching the school bus at his mother's house
at that time. He took a breath. A really deep one. And
then he spoke. "You accessed Grandma's laptop?"

Vangie made a little face of acknowledgment. "Her
phone, actually."

His heart began to race because he knew that all-
too-innocent look she was giving him. It was the same
wide-eyed expression he'd used to wrangle himself out
of a great many things over the years. "Evangeline Mary
Moyer, what on earth have you done?"

"Daddy." She spoke with an ever-patient, exasperat-
ing, yet still adorable, air. "I'm going to find you a wife."

Tug Moyer looked shocked.

No, make that dumbfounded, which annoyed Christa
Alero even more. First he trained a child on how to make
videos, then had the nerve to be surprised when she did it.

What a dolt. No matter how amazingly good-looking
the guy was, with his shock of brown hair, ruddy-brown
eyes and a heart-stopping, to-die-for grin, he was foolish
to take such liberties with children. He was a cop. More
than anyone, he should know how easy it would be for the
wrong kind of person to see Evangeline's plea, be taken
with the child and then do something stupid or dangerous.
Wasn't the world already perilous enough for children?

She should know. She'd grown up in the thick of it.

She choked the negativity down. She'd dealt with
her past years before. She might not be able to change
what had happened, but she could smooth the road she'd
chosen. She'd become a teacher to influence the future
and that meant everything.

"My office. Now." The principal didn't mince words. She stepped back and waved one hand. "After you."

Deputy Moyer and his really cute daughter went on ahead.

Christa fell in step with the principal. Halfway down the hall, she glanced to her left.

A tiny smile softened the principal's features, as if she thought either the incident or the pair in front of them were amusing. Or worse, endearing. Clearly she liked the guy.

I'm going to find you a wife.

Evangeline's words and her winning smile weren't lost on Christa. Appealing, yes. But dangerous when paired with the social-media frenzy.

Christa took a seat on the far left, facing the principal. The deputy took the seat in the middle. Evangeline sat to his right.

Was he protecting the girl by opting for the middle seat? Or was he trying to intimidate Christa?

Or he could just be sitting... Like a normal person.

The mental scolding was right. Being raised in a gang-infested California city where too many cops looked the other way tended to ignite her suspicions. She took a breath and quietly folded her hands in her lap. The principal would handle this. That took the onus off Christa and helped ensure an ongoing good relationship with the child.

Mrs. Menendez took her seat. "Tug, you know this is serious."

Tug?

Christa bit back words of recrimination because calling the guy by a nickname leveled the playing field too quickly. He should have to suffer more, shouldn't he?

"It is gravely serious," he replied. He aimed a ridiculously handsome look at his daughter and she wriggled under the scrutiny. "Vangie, you know better than this. It's dangerous for kids to be on the internet. You took a big chance that bad people might see you or your brother. Most people are going to think your post is cute. That's why it's been shared…" He swept a look at his phone. His eyes went wide and it was impossible to miss the gorgeous tones of cinnamon brown. "Nearly three million times now."

"We have local TV stations and national news networks calling for interviews," the principal told him. "I'm sure you'll find similar circumstances at home."

"National news?" His voice cracked. Just a little. She hadn't thought his gorgeous eyes could go wider. Wrong.

Mrs. Menendez pressed her lips together and nodded.

"I thought just some nice people around here would see it," Vangie piped up. "You never get a chance to go out with ladies, Dad. You're always helping other people or saving lives, and how are you ever going to find a wife if you never look? Especially if you get to be the new sheriff. So I thought this would help."

Christa almost choked.

The child was delightfully smart and utterly sincere.

"Vangie, I know you meant well, but this isn't how it's done, honey."

Evangeline almost bounced in her seat as she argued her point. "It is, Dad! Maybe that's the problem because it's *exactly* how they do it now. There are so many people on social media and they love stories like this. I heard Grandma and Nurse Mortie talking about it. She said people absolutely eat this stuff up."

The principal choked back a laugh and even Christa had to fight a smile because the girl's sincerity was spot-on.

"Eavesdropping on grown-up conversations, then taking that information and deliberately disobeying our rules isn't something I take lightly, Evangeline." He was firm. Strong. Direct. And the uniform added an extra measure of power to drive his points home.

The girl gulped.

The deputy turned and made eye contact with the adults. "Ms. Alero and Mrs. Menendez, I apologize for today's disruption. With the soaring numbers of this post, I can't promise it won't stay a nuisance for a while. If you'd like me to keep Evangeline home, I can do that. She can stay with my mother while I work."

"And miss school?" Evangeline's eyes went wide. She turned to the principal quickly. "We can't do that. You know how much I love school, Mrs. M.!"

Another nickname, which meant the rules of school decorum might not be very rigid in Golden Grove.

"And we all appreciate your enthusiasm and scholarly efforts, Vangie, but the school isn't equipped to handle prying people or—"

The school secretary buzzed in right then. "Mrs. Menendez, I'm sorry to interrupt, but we have a developing situation. Reporters are clogging the bus loop. The buses can't pull in to pick up the students. There are sheriff's deputies arriving to help straighten things out, but I thought you should be aware."

Reporters. Law-enforcement response en masse. All for a little girl who should have been watched more carefully.

The injustice of it rose up to choke Christa.

She knew the inequalities of police response. She'd seen it firsthand. Little help came her way back in Sinclair, California, but up here in small-town Washington State, a cute kid makes a heart-wrenching video and cops come out of the woodwork to keep her safe and sound.

The disparity triggered too many old hurts. Where was all this help when a teenage girl found herself in desperate situations thirteen years ago?

Fortunately, Evangeline was a pleasure to have in class, and Christa would only have to see the clueless father a few times over the course of the year. She could handle that. She stood. "I've got to get back to my class for dismissal. *If* the buses can safely access the children, that is."

The deputy rose out of his chair, too.

He didn't loom, although he could have because he was a good six inches taller than she was. He turned her way. "Ms. Alero, I'm sorry our first meeting was like this. Evangeline is normally—" he slanted a gaze at his daughter "—well behaved. And a hard worker. You can be sure I'll follow through with this at home."

She appreciated the sincere promise. She nodded quickly. "Thank you, Deputy Moyer."

She started to turn but had to stop when a shorter, older man in uniform strode into the room. He stood inside, crossed his arms and held the taller cop's gaze. "This is a debacle and just a few months before my retirement, Tug. I was hoping for a quiet fall, but I guess not."

The deputy's boss?

She spotted the name tag that read Sheriff Wainwright and she almost felt sorry for Evangeline's father.

"It is, sir. We'll see that it gets fixed." That was the deputy's response, but he didn't seem all that concerned.

"We've got the bus loop handled," the sheriff continued, "but with the outpouring of media and the growing unrest in the middle school, the school council and I have made a decision."

The deputy kept his face flat as he asked, "A decision?"

"Tug, you're great with kids," said the sheriff. "You're one of the best officers we've got, and you know I have to pull you off patrol after today's incident. One of us needs to follow protocol. In this case, it's me."

The deputy acknowledged that with a twitch of his mouth, and Christa did not want to think how engaging that particular move was. Not following the rules made him a rule breaker, too, she realized. Clearly the apple didn't fall far from the tree.

"We're reassigning you to the school district temporarily. You'll be the Golden Grove resource officer for a while. That way we've addressed security issues at the school, and the rise in gang affiliation with the kids in a few of the rougher areas."

"Dad!" Evangeline grabbed hold of his hand. "Does that mean you'll work right here? With me and Nathan? Won't that be so absolutely perfect?"

Christa's emotions rose all over again. She couldn't

believe that the county was naming a resource officer to the schools because a cute kid posted a video.

The lack of equitability sent a slow burn up her back.

They'd had a few guards at Sinclair City High, and each one of them had turned their back on a whole lot of stuff that went down in those halls. Stuff that had changed her life.

She took a step toward the door. "Excuse me."

The sheriff smiled at her and stepped aside, but then he offered his hand. "You're new here, aren't you? Welcome to Golden Grove, Ms. Alero. Mrs. Menendez shared your credentials with the board and we worried that a bigger district might win the day, so we were very happy when you chose us."

She accepted the kind gesture. "Thank you, Sheriff. My aunt lives somewhere in this area, and she loved the location. I haven't had time to connect with her yet, but it will be nice to become reacquainted. We haven't seen each other in over fifteen years."

"Family's a good thing."

She hoped so.

Her mother had kicked her aunt out of the house when Christa was twelve. They'd emigrated from Guatemala before Christa was born. Her mother had come to America to give her three-year-old sister and her unborn child a chance at a new life. She'd sacrificed so much to offer a clear, clean future, but neither she nor her aunt had respected that as a teen.

Christa was sorry for that now. It was too late to make it up to her late mother, but maybe she and Marta could make a difference together. She eased out the door and started toward her classroom.

"Ms. Alero."

That voice. Kind, yet commanding.

She'd seen the election posters that had popped up around town the past few days. Now she could put a face to the Tug Moyer for Sheriff signs dotting many front lawns.

Evangeline's good-looking father wasn't only a local deputy. He was running for county sheriff, and that position could make him privy to all kinds of information. Like why she had a juvenile record back in California.

She turned and looked at him.

He met her gaze with such a sincere expression that her heart almost melted, but not quite. "Yes?"

He fell into step beside her, as if he cared that she was needed in her classroom and didn't want to hold her up. "I truly am sorry about this. Impressed, too." He slanted her a grin and she had to work hard to ignore the way her heart jumped again. "Vangie's a quick learner, and I'm her project-of-the-day, it seems."

The fairly laid-back assessment tweaked her. "Project-of-the-day?"

"In her quest for total world domination, my daughter is pretty sure she can fix things if people would simply listen to her."

His frank words drew her smile. "A lady boss."

The title deepened the laugh lines around his eyes. "Exactly. And it will be fine with me when she moves on from the current quest because I'm pretty much a lost cause in the romance department."

She was about to do a mental eye roll because that was about the cheesiest line she'd ever heard, and she'd heard her share over the last few years...

But then he went on.

"We lost her mom three years ago."

The revelation sparked her sympathy. "I'm so sorry."

He acknowledged her words with a look of appreciation. "Thank you. I won't pretend it's been easy, but other than the current debacle," he added frankly as they neared her door, "we're doing all right on our own. And while I hate to disappoint my resident matchmaker, that's how it's going to stay. I've got enough on my plate. As you can plainly see."

They'd reached her classroom.

She paused.

So did he.

And when she looked up and met his gaze, she read the sorrow and sincerity there, and that expression was enough to make her wish he'd give romance a second chance.

Chapter Two

Tug's mother had texted him that their house was surrounded by reporters from all over the Pacific Northwest. He could either face them now or face them tomorrow when his work was done and he'd had time to sleep. The thought of saying something stupid that might cost him the election made the decision for him.

Tomorrow won.

He drove toward the O'Laughlins' apple farm, then pulled into what used to be Libby Creighton's driveway. Libby had gotten married last year, and the hands-on exhibit farm was already knee-deep in early-September apples, but no one would expect the Moyers to be staying in the vacant bungalow-style home. The press had staked themselves outside his house and his parents' place. His parents had sold their farm to a major fruit conglomerate after his dad's heart attack, but their former orchard abutted the O'Laughlins'. Once a neighbor in Central Washington, always a neighbor. It was a good place to hide in plain sight. He was glad his mother had thought to call Libby and arrange things so they could avoid the onslaught of sudden interest in his private life.

His aunt Grace was waiting at the side door. "I know you've got things to do," she told him as the kids hopped out of the unmarked car he'd borrowed from the station. "I'll watch these guys tonight. We've got folks going in and out of your parents' house to keep the press occupied."

"Decoys? Mom's idea, I expect."

"Always looking out for folks," Grace told him with a laugh. "Two morning shows are already requesting interviews. And I expect there will be plenty more."

That brought his chin up after kissing the kids goodbye. "Interviews?"

"I forgot." She waved her hands as she talked, totally animated 24/7. "You're never around to see the morning news. They love anything nice that goes viral. It might be something to think about. It could be a great shout-out for your teen ministry. That's if we don't kill Vangie first," she added cheerfully as the eight-year-old hurried by her. "That would change the story, I expect."

"Auntie…" Vangie tipped the sweetest of smiles up to her aunt. "Really?"

"Oh, we'll let you live, darling, but only because you are a delightful package of beauty, brains and tenacity, and I happen to like all three," Grace assured her. "I'll leave the scolding to others because I loved that video, Evangeline. I may have shared it a few times myself."

"Aunt Grace." Tug frowned purposely, but had to bite back a grin.

"Go on in, you two," Grace directed the kids. "I'll be right there. I made mac and cheese for supper," she

continued once the kids were out of earshot. "I'm keeping them inside tonight even though it's nice out. Just
so no one happens to see Evangeline and notifies the
press. Libby's at the old barn up the road and she said
we can use the house as long as we need to." Libby and
her husband, Jax McClaren, had turned her family farm
into an old-fashioned hands-on facility over the past
year. In the middle of huge commercial fruit farms and
orchards, O'Laughlin Farms offered folks a chance to
step back into simpler times.

"I'm grateful." Things would die down eventually.
They always did, but the outpouring of affection for
Vangie's plea was astronomical. Now he needed to keep
everyone safe—including his own children—while reporters and strangers milled around their small town.
And while he considered both sides of his new school
assignment. "I'm going to the station house to take care
of some paperwork. I'll be back soon."

"I've got this," Aunt Grace said.

He knew she did. He was blessed with great family.
His wife Hadley's parents had relocated to Arizona before she'd passed away, but his whole family loved being
part of the kids' lives. It meant a lot to him to have his
children surrounded by so much love.

Tug called Jubilee Samson's number as he drove to
the station, then asked about the boys when the social
worker answered. "It's Tug Moyer, Jubilee. How are the
little guys doing?"

"Well enough," she replied. "The hospital is releasing them to an emergency foster-care placement for
overnight and I'm searching for family. Jeremy's hanging in there, but little Jonah is beside himself. He just

keeps crying for his mama and no one seems to know where she is."

That could mean several things. If the kids were the children of an undocumented immigrant, the paper trail thinned quickly. And finding them with an addict who had a long rap sheet wasn't normal. No one would intentionally leave their children with someone like that. Given the circumstances, he'd be surprised if their mother turned up happy and whole anywhere, and that thought made him sad. "Was the guy with the gun their father?"

"No," she replied. "And no trace of the mother. He didn't make it, by the way."

Tug sighed. He loved his job, but he didn't love that kind of outcome. Losing someone to anger or depression or desperation never sat right, even when the guy had a fairly lengthy criminal record.

"But you and Renzo got the boys out before the guy turned the gun," she continued.

Renzo Calloway was his partner and best friend. Long before they'd become deputy sheriffs, they'd been joined in friendship as both sets of their parents reached out to foster kids throughout the county. Tug's parents paused their fostering efforts when his father developed a heart problem, but Renzo's mother had taken on orphaned triplets a few years before. Vangie and Nathan thought the identical girls were an oddity at first. But now they were just three kids who happened to look alike.

"You saved the boys' lives," Jubilee added. "You did good, Tug."

Something to thank God for, right there. It broke his

heart to have little children involved in death and disaster. Children were so special. So dear. Each one a gift from God. "I wish we could save everyone, Jubilee."

"That poor soul had a long history with the Quincy police, according to what I've seen. He's been on the down side of life and the high side of drugs for a long time. How he ended up in that house with those little ones is anyone's guess. I'm hoping this was an aberration and that their mother shows up healthy and whole."

Would a mother who loved her children leave them in that situation? Tug couldn't imagine it, but that was a topic for another day. "Keep me posted, okay? I want to make sure they're safe and sound and together." Recently it had been difficult to find families willing to take multiple kids for foster-care placement. The Calloways and the Moyers had always been exceptions to that rule. If these little fellows were brothers, he didn't want to see them separated.

He filled out the required forms at the station house as he considered appropriate forms of punishment for Evangeline. *Except...*

Her little ruse amazed him. Yes, she'd created a spectacle. He knew she didn't comprehend the far-reaching effects of social media. She saw the thousands of likes and shares on his posts, but a girl her age couldn't comprehend these out-of-the-stratosphere numbers on his social-media account. He'd never had one of his videos snowball like this.

For a kid her age to have that much gumption and initiative was mind-boggling. It was wrong, yes. But how many eight-year-olds could execute a plan like that in the thirty minutes she and her brother were at their grandparents' house this morning?

The kid showed promise. It was kind of a shame to clip her wings, but he was the parent. Therefore, that fell into his wheelhouse.

Aunt Grace called a few minutes later. "I promised the monsters they could say good-night to you."

He laughed. So did they. Nathan burbled with joy, such a happy child. And Vangie had already moved on to something else after watching a nature show about the effects of plastic on sea waters. She'd worked on fixing his marital status that morning. Now she was ready to protect the world's oceans. All in a day's work, it seemed.

He loved them. He loved them so much that he couldn't imagine life without them. Hadley had left them far too soon. She'd lost out on years of hugs and kisses, so when he did those things, he did them for two. Every embrace and cherished moment wasn't just for him, but for their mama in Heaven. A woman who was too busy to take care of herself because he was too busy being cop-of-the-year.

He tamped down the guilt that threatened to over-flow from deep inside him.

Tomorrow he'd check on the boys again. Make sure they were all right. When he'd plowed through the pile of paperwork related to their case, he grabbed a burger at a drive-through in Quincy, ate it on his way home and pulled into the small parking area outside the O'Laughlin farmhouse.

He hadn't been followed. He'd checked deliberately. If he could get a good night's sleep, he'd tackle report-

ers in the morning. He hugged his aunt, sent her on her
way and slept on the comfy sofa in the living room. He'd
don his superhero uniform first thing in the morning,
but for tonight…

Tonight he slept.

Christa steered her car around the throngs of reporters lining the street and eased into a space in the
teacher's parking area. Deputies had moved the reporters off school grounds, so it wasn't quite the fiasco
they'd faced yesterday. She was grateful for that. As
she stepped out of the car and took a deep breath of
fresh, clean country air, she realized there was a whole
list of things to thank God for up here.

Central Washington wasn't like any other place she'd
known. While she'd never lived in a small town, she
was pretty sure she'd fallen in love the first day she
got here, and that was an amazing feeling. Once she
settled in, she'd make a concerted effort to find her
aunt Marta. The Quincy address Marta had sent years
ago had been a dead end, and there hadn't been time
to delve further while starting her new job and setting
up her classroom, but she'd give it a try this weekend.
If Marta still lived here, Christa wanted the chance to
get to know her, without all the drama that had surrounded them as youngsters. Was it silly to long for a
nice, normal American family existence, like the ones
she saw on TV?

She hoped not.

She slung her heavy canvas teaching bag over her
head and shoulder, then lifted the science box from her
back seat as an SUV backed in next to her. She had no

free hands, so she hip-checked the door to close it, then moved forward.

Her neck jerked back.

The full book bag slid backward, weighing her down. When she tried to loosen the weight on her throat by taking her right hand off the heavy box, the box tipped precariously.

She tried pulling at the strap to ease the strain.

That maneuver only tightened the noose around her neck, and she couldn't bend low enough to set the science box down. Dropping it was out of the question. She'd spent nearly two-hundred-and-fifty dollars on those microscopes and lenses. They wouldn't survive the fall to the asphalt. But she was trapped by the closed, locked door that had caught her strap, with no way to get her key fob to unlock it unless she dropped the box.

"Oh, this isn't good."

That voice again, a ripe blend of amusement and chagrin.

"Hang on, Ms. Alero. Let me take the box. Vangie, hold your brother's hand and go straight into the school."

"Okay, Daddy."

Tug didn't just lift the box from her hands. He realized instantly that the strap was choking her and he slid one big, strong hand beneath the tightly woven canvas strap and pulled it toward him to release the strain on her throat while he grabbed the science box with his left hand. Spiced aftershave made her long to draw closer. Breathe deeper. But the current predicament made both impossible, which was probably a good thing. He gripped and pulled the canvas strap a little farther. "Can you duck under?"

She couldn't find her voice to say yes. She nodded and slipped beneath the strap. Then she grabbed her key from her pocket and hit the unlock button on the fob. A pain shot through her chest when she tried to draw a breath.

That surprised her, but when she realized how short the free end of the strap was, she understood why she'd been gasping for air. She jerked the door open.

The snagged strap fell free. She closed the door again, hit the lock button and turned.

Whoa.

He was watching her with worried eyes. Eyes that went straight to the heart and maybe even the soul. Eyes that drew her even more than the spiced autumn scent surrounding her.

"That was a close call, ma'am." Concern deepened his gaze further. "If I was setting up an accidental death scene, I would never have thought about this particular combination."

The *ma'am* was cute. Colloquial. Like old-time Mayberry stuff. It would be so easy to flirt with him. See how much of that charisma was genuine. But she hadn't come to town with the goal of ruining someone's political career, and new sheriffs and old felons weren't a good mix, and he'd already made his lack of options known. End of story.

"You could have dropped the box." He raised the container slightly. "Things are replaceable. You aren't."

"Too much invested in that box," she replied as she pulled the bag back up. She didn't feed the strap over her head this time. Over her shoulder would be good enough. Her voice rasped slightly when she spoke. The sound made him frown.

"That strangle did a number on you. You should go to the nurse," he advised. He fell into step beside her, and even though the entire crowd of reporters was shouting his name and pressing against the police tape that someone had erected to keep them off school property, he kept his gaze on her and still managed to get the door open with his free hand without glancing away. "What if it did internal damage or something?"

"I'm fine." She took a deep cleansing breath and the next words came easier. "Just a little shaken that something like that could happen. I would have never imagined it. Thank you, Deputy."

"Tug," he told her. "Just doing my job." He brushed it off as if he went around saving people from rogue bag straps on a regular basis. He winked and smiled, which only managed to send her thoughts straight back to the flirting that couldn't possibly happen, while he saluted Mrs. Harrington at the main entrance desk. "Good morning, Miss Ivy."

The elderly woman hurried around the curved desk and threw her arms around him. "Tug, I'm thrilled that you're going to be working here! There's a group over at the middle school that bears watching. They've been trying to mess with some of our fifth and sixth graders, and not much has been done."

"Mrs. Menendez told me about the gang symbols in the boys' bathrooms," he replied. "I'll keep my eye on things. We'll figure out what's going on and see what we can do to stop it."

"Riffraff from the coast, that's what's going on," complained the old woman. "Bringing drugs to small towns. It's not right, Tug. It's just not right."

Christa didn't stick around to hear his reply, because she was some of that coastal riffraff. It wasn't wrong for a town to protect itself, but was this a common assumption here? That everyone who came from a troubled past was suspect?

She'd broken free with the help and inspiration of some wonderful teachers. Now she wanted to do the same for others. This section of Central Washington had a more diverse population than the state as a whole. Here she could begin anew and inspire children. That was her goal.

Broad footsteps followed her down the hall. She didn't have to turn to know who was approaching. When she turned into her classroom, Evangeline's eyes lit up. "Daddy!"

He came in behind Christa, set the science box down, then hugged his daughter. "You be good, smart and respectful because right now I have to go outside and face those reporters, young lady."

She peeked up at him, guilty.

"And then I'll be here on school grounds for the foreseeable future. Here's my cell number." He raised his gaze to include Christa as he handed her a slip of paper. "Just in case."

The hot cop's cell number.

The born romantic in her loved the notion.

The pragmatic woman with a record knew better.

But when he touched his daughter's head and said, "I love you, Vangie. You are the very best of your mama and me put together, and she'd be proud of your initiative," she heard the longing in his voice.

And that touched her even more than his magnificent smile.

Chapter Three

"Here he comes!"

A female voice announced Tug's appearance as he crossed the wide driveway leading to the school's drop-off areas. A host of voices began hurling questions his way, and when it seemed more like mayhem than an interview, he raised his hands for quiet.

Surprisingly, most of them hushed up. "I have ten minutes," he told them. "Let's not waste them. I'm sure you've all got the basics on me because it's public record, so let's start with you." He motioned toward a middle-aged woman with short spiky hair.

"Two questions," she announced briskly. "One, do you intend to let your daughter live—"

A soft chorus of laughter rolled through the group of reporters.

"And two, why would a sheriff train a child on how to use a dangerous instrument like the internet?"

"She's alive and well thus far," he replied and didn't soften the droll note to his voice. "And while I didn't train her, I did teach her how to shoot videos to send to her grandparents who live out of town. That way they stay in touch with her visually. The ease of social media did the rest because my mother had my vlogging app on her phone."

"For your teen-empowerment videos?"

"Correct."

"Are you searching for a wife, Deputy?"

That came from a man a little farther back, and the entire group seemed to wait for his reply. He gave them a rueful grin as he scrubbed a hand to the back of his neck. "I'm not."

"And yet we have a list of women who would love to meet you," stated a local reporter. She raised a sheet of paper in her free hand. He recognized her from the midday news that was often on in the station-house break room.

"Please tell me you're kidding."

She made a face at him. "Not kidding. And some of the comments have gone viral, as well. You've become a meme."

He'd thought this couldn't get worse.

It just had.

"There are worse things I could be, I suppose. But I had not figured on being a meme, so that's something new."

"Deputy," a middle-aged man he didn't recognize called out from the back of the group. "There is speculation that you put her up to this to garner more local votes in the November election. Is there a grain of truth in that? The timing does make it suspicious."

The hairs along the back of Tug's neck stood up.

No one who knew him, or Evangeline, would think

that, but Ross Converse, the other candidate for sheriff, liked to throw shade. Ross was fairly new to the Columbia Plateau area. He'd been a police chief near Seattle, then moved inland three years ago. He quickly became known for his I-know-best summations at local governmental meetings and didn't seem to understand that Central Washington folks didn't always appreciate being told what to do by outsiders. He'd stirred up a lot of negative discussion lately, and now he was running for sheriff. It didn't make a lot of sense to Tug, but he met the reporter's gaze and shrugged. "A man can't control what folks might say, but I'm going to let my record as a deputy sheriff and unit commander speak for itself. I know a lot of these voters. They're smart people and I'd never insult their intelligence by rigging an attention-grabbing scheme."

"Deputy, we'd love to have you on WPAB," cut in another woman. "I know you've gotten lots of interview requests, but it would be wonderful to have the local stations get the scoop."

"I'm a scoop?" He flashed a grin. "I'm taking all requests seriously, but right now I have a job that I take even more seriously, and as you can see—" he motioned toward the school as a chorus of village church bells announced the eight o'clock hour "—my workday has begun. Thank you all."

He ignored the clamor of voices that followed. He could reconvene with them later, but right now, he needed to meet with the principals and design a game plan that kept him in proximity to all three schools despite the spacious layout that left room for high-school athletic fields.

He wanted the administrators' trust and to trust them in return, but by the end of the day he realized that the junior-high principal was too busy trying to be the kids' friend to be an effective leader. Was the middle school's spike in problem behaviors and lack of proficiency due to her ineptitude? Or because there was a bad crop of kids in the current seventh- and eighth-grade classes?

He let himself into the east wing of the elementary school for a quick meeting with Mrs. Menendez as the buses pulled out that afternoon. The first thing he heard was a grief-stricken child. The little one was sobbing as if his or her little heart would break, and Tug hurried in that direction.

Jubilee Samson came around the corner right then. She had one little boy in her arms. He was the one crying, his sweet face buried against her shoulder.

The other boy spotted Tug and recognized him from their interaction the previous day. "Hey!" he yelled. He jerked free of Jubilee's hand and raced toward Tug. "Hey, you! Hey!"

He didn't just grab Tug. He leaped into his arms as if searching for safety or salvation or something the least bit familiar. "You're the copper guy. You're the copper guy!"

"Deputy," he told the boy as he hugged him. "From yesterday, right?"

"I remember. I remember!"

And even though the standoff ended well for the boys, Tug hoped the memory would fade in time. He held the boy and met Jubilee's gaze over his head. "What's up? Do we have news?"

Her grave expression shared silent consternation.

"I've come to see Ms. Alero. She teaches third grade here."

"Evangeline's teacher." He said the words as Christa came their way from the bus loop. He motioned her over. "This is Ms. Alero, Jubilee."

The social worker turned. Then she turned back toward Tug. "Tug, I'm sure you're busy, but can you watch the boys for a few minutes while I speak to Ms. Alero?"

"Sure." He took the crying boy from her, then crossed the hall and opened the door to a kindergarten room. "Fellas. Let's see what they've got in here."

The littlest boy's distress broke the deputy's heart. Tug was a fixer. A negotiator. A guardian. Right now, all of his skills came to the surface. He guided the older boy into the room and quietly shut the door.

Normal little fellows would have scrambled around the room, checking things out.

Not these two.

The littlest one clung to him with his tousled head burrowed into Tug's shoulder. The older boy—Jeremy—took a seat on a little chair and folded his hands. Eyes down, he sat there, alone and despondent, as if nothing could ever be right again.

Tug took a breath.

He didn't have the words to fix whatever disaster had impacted these two little lives, but he had a few skill sets that had sat untapped once Nathan and Vangie went to school.

Without releasing his grip on little Jonah, he began singing a popular kids' song. When the boys' tears turned to watery smiles, he breathed a little sigh of relief.

* * *

Marta gone?

And the guy who'd held those two precious children hostage yesterday, two boys who were her baby cousins, was Marta's newest boyfriend and drug supplier, according to the social worker. And he was gone, too.

Christa sank into her chair in disbelief.

The social worker dragged up a folding chair by the reading circle and set it down beside her. "I'm sorry I had to be the one to tell you. The police chief in Quincy offered to deliver the news, but our office was already involved because of the boys. Ms. Alero…" The middle-aged woman sighed softly. "I'm so dreadfully sorry. Were you and your aunt close?"

Christa shook her head. It took a long moment for her to find her words because of the torrent of emotions swirling within her.

Marta had been so funny, so pretty. They'd been girls together, before Marta took up with one of the leaders of the Santiago gang in Sinclair. There'd only been three years between them, which meant Marta would have been thirty now.

If she'd lived.

The disbelief rose up again. "Are you sure you have the right person? That it is my aunt Marta? And that these children are hers?"

The woman's expression deepened. She nodded and gripped her hands together as if in prayer. At this moment, Christa would welcome the prayers and all the help she could get, because how does a person handle grief upon grief?

One step at a time…

She'd learned that the hard way, but what if one got tired of stepping?

"We are certain." The social worker leaned forward. "And it was by the grace of God we found you so quickly. His grace and the internet because her name was linked to yours. And to a Margaretta Alero, in California. Imagine my surprise when I plugged your name into the system and realized you'd just moved here. The Lord works in mysterious ways," she finished softly. Then she noted the small cross hanging on the thin chain around Christa's neck. "You probably already know that."

Did she?

Some days. But during the dark times when she'd railed against her mother, when she'd run amok in anger, when she blamed her mother for Marta's departure, it wasn't God's ways she followed. He didn't deal in ways of darkness and deceit. How she wished she'd known that back then.

"I know this is a shock, but state law says that family placement takes precedence over foster care for bereft children, and I wanted to see how you felt about that."

The boys.

She'd spotted them in the hallway. One safe in the clutches of the deputy's arms, and one looking so very lost and alone. "They'll need a home."

"Yes. But don't feel that you have to take on more than you're capable of, Ms. Alero. We can find temporary placement for them, if need be."

Shuffled off to strangers, like so many of the kids she'd grown up with. Surrounded by whomever, and good or bad, it wouldn't be family. It wouldn't be the people who should love them best. "I only have a little studio apartment. Not nearly enough room…"

"I understand." The woman—Jubilee—didn't pressure her. "I'll find a spot for them, and—"

"No." Christa drew herself up, surprised. "No, that's not what I meant. Not at all what I meant. They are family, these boys. *Mis primos*," she went on. "My cousins. They will stay with me, of course, but the lack of space makes it hard."

"There's space at my parents' place." Tug Moyer's voice interrupted them from behind. The social worker turned quickly.

"Tug, your parents have helped a lot of kids over the years. Would they be willing?"

"Deputy, I—"

Christa started to interject, but paused when he came forward. He hooked a thumb across the way as he pulled another chair forward. "Mrs. Menendez is with the boys now. They're pretty shaken up."

Who wouldn't be? And to be such little fellows, besides?

He sat, pressed his hands together and leaned forward to get her attention. He got it, all right. The strength of his manner, the sincerity of his gaze said this was the kind of man you could count on.

"Ms. Alero, my parents have been foster parents for nearly two decades. They've got a good-sized house, and room for you and the boys to stay together until you find somewhere else to move. If nothing else, it buys you time right now. Time to wrap your head around all of this. To adjust. To grieve."

His expression said more and she remembered his

look that morning, a mix of sorrow and guilt. A look she identified with because that same expression looked back at her from the mirror, every single day.

"They've got plenty of space and my mom might be available to watch the boys during the day while you work. At least for the time being."

"You can't possibly speak for her."

He cringed slightly, but more in amusement than angst. "You'll understand when you meet her. She is affectionately known as Hurricane Darla and generally sweeps in like a Category Four. She's got a heart for children. Vangie and Nathan go there every day after school. I expect they'd love to see the boys."

What could she say?

The Lord giveth. The Lord taketh away. Blessed be the name of the Lord.

Was that how it really worked or did bad stuff just happen and humans learned to adapt or not?

She wasn't sure, but to have so many things fall into place… That meant something, didn't it?

She took a deep breath. Stood up. Then she stretched out a hand to Tug Moyer. "I will accept your offer on behalf of your parents. If they are half as kind as their son, then I know we'll be in good hands until we find a bigger place."

"I'll let them know."

He took her hand. Held it. And for those brief moments, she wasn't sure where her hand began and where his left off.

Not magic, like in the movies.

But belonging. As if destiny did have a say in things.

And yet she understood the levels of impossible more than most.

She'd committed a crime in California. She had a record. Sure, it was supposed to be sealed, but was it? Really? This guy, this kind, gracious and bighearted man, was running for county sheriff, and there was no way in the world she was going to let this attraction ruin his job or his life.

But when he gave her hand the gentlest squeeze of compassion, she realized something else.

It was going to be nearly impossible not to fall for him, so that meant she had her work cut out for her. Fortunately, she'd been a sci-fi fan as a youthful reader. All she needed now was a cozy home and a cloak of invisibility and she'd be all set.

Chapter Four

The pizza delivery girl couldn't get through the throng of press that surrounded his parents' house. Tug called a neighbor on the next block, and when the neighbor texted him that the pizza was delivered, they did the exchange over the backyard fence. "Thanks, Mike."

His parents' neighbor waved it off. "Glad to help. This internet stuff gets out of hand, doesn't it?"

Tug was just about to agree when Mike added, "Although my sister's got a daughter who's single, Tug. Real nice gal. Kind of shy. Never married. Just needs to meet the right guy."

If Tug had a nickel for everyone who casually mentioned a single friend, sister, daughter, neighbor, waitress...

He slipped back into the house through the back door, glad for the help of neighbors but wishing folks would leave his lack of a love life alone. It simply wasn't anyone else's business.

"That smells great." Vangie was curled up in his father's recliner as he passed by. She was already halfway through a book she'd started that morning, but the enticing smell of food drew her quick interest. "I forgot I was hungry."

"A good book will do that to you." He moved into the kitchen as Christa came down the stairs. He indicated the box as he slid the pizza onto the counter. "Sustenance. How are the boys doing?"

She folded her arms as if cold, but the room was warm. Then her brows drew down. "Your mom is reading to them, and I honestly don't know how to answer that question. Will they ever be all right? Even if the rest of their lives are peaceful, how do kids get over something like this?"

He didn't pretend it wasn't a concern. "I see a lot of sad stories in my job."

She held his gaze and blinked once. "Me, too."

"Mom and Dad have helped over a dozen kids regain a hold on life when things went downhill, so I've seen it work. And in this case, with Jeremy and Jonah, they've got you." He splayed his hands. "That's huge, Ms. Alero."

"Christa. Please."

"A real pretty name." A perfect match to its lovely owner.

The compliment eased the tension in her face. "Thank you."

"They're young," he continued. He kept his voice low so the boys wouldn't overhear them. "Do you recall anything from before you were five or so?"

Her brow knit, then smoothed. "Not really."

"So maybe that will be the case for them, too," he continued. "I'm not saying that having your mother disappear and a rough first couple of years might not

44   *Learning to Trust*

have an effect, but I think that can be minimized with faith, hope and love. And the greatest of these is love."

Her brow furrowed again. When it did, he was pretty sure she'd had too much practice being worried and a part of him wanted to reach out. Smooth that brow. Let her know she wasn't in this alone. He shoved the random thought aside as she glanced toward the stairs. "It's a lot to take in."

"To hear the news about family and then have two little kids thrust on you," he acknowledged. "It sure is."

She shook her head quickly. "No, not that. I'm strong. I'm not afraid of a challenge. And I love kids. That's why I chose a career in teaching.

"I mean for them," she explained. "To take in a new place, new people, new toys. When people buy a puppy, the breeders often give them a blanket with the mother's scent on it to comfort the pup as he adjusts. These boys have nothing. Do we even know where they were living?" she asked. "Would it be possible to see if they have any belongings we could salvage? Just to have something familiar in their lives?"

"My guess is it wasn't all that sudden," he said softly. "But, yes, we'll see if there's anything we can find. Jubilee thinks Marta probably became homeless a couple of months back. When the choice is drugs or rent money, the rent money often takes a back seat. But they must have been somewhere. We'll check it out."

"Thank you. Your mother's reading them a story about a bear and all his friends."

"That is like one of my favoritest stories in the whole world!" Nathan slid into the room in sock-clad feet, and saved himself from colliding with the table by crashing into Tug. "And Grandma reads it the best. She can do all the animal voices," Nathan went on as he zeroed in on the pizza. "Can we eat now? Because I'm like so really hungry, Dad. Like almost starving." He widened his eyes and gave a fairly convincing little boy groan for effect.

Tug's father came in from outside as Nathan clutched his middle. "Sounds good to me. I'll wash up quick and we can say grace. Mom upstairs?"

Tug nodded. "Reading to the boys. Should we wait for her?"

"Well, here's the truth about having two cute little kids." Glenn Moyer shot them an over-the-shoulder knowing look as he scrubbed up. "Eating in shifts becomes the norm. Sure, it's great when you can all sit around a table, and that will come in time, but for now, meal shifts are a wonderful thing. That way the boys aren't thrust into any more expectations than they need and we get hot food."

"Mom would love your reasoning."

"*Love* might be a strong word," his father teased. "But she'd go along with it. Christa, I want you to know that you and the boys are welcome to be here as long as you need to be," he said as he dried his hands. "I also understand that you probably cherish your privacy, so if you need help looking for a place of your own, just give us a heads-up. We don't want to intrude, and we don't want you to feel pushed out. We know there aren't a lot of available rentals in small towns like this. Over in Quincy, yes."

Tug read her instant frown. "You want to stay more rural."

"Yes." She folded her hands but it was more of a clench. "I was raised in a city. Nothing about it was good in my case, so coming here was my ticket to freedom. If you don't mind us being here long enough for me to find something in town, I would be grateful. I don't mind paying rent, either. I like paying my own way," she added firmly.

"You're already doing that until you sublet your studio above the pharmacy, although I expect Mr. Johannson will let you out of your lease," Tug told her. "He's a good guy."

"You think so?" That thought smoothed some of her worry furrow. "That would be a huge relief on me and my budget."

"If you explain the circumstances, he'll understand, and that place rents out the minute it becomes available, being right in town like that. And he keeps it up nicely." He reached over and slid a chair out for her as Vangie came into the room.

"I got to a great stopping place in the book, but then that means that the beginning of the next chapter is a great starting place, so can I eat fast and read for twenty more minutes since there are no dishes tonight? Please?"

"*May* I eat fast, and why should tonight be any different?" Tug slid out a chair for her, too. "Chew your food, wait until we say grace, and then I want to hear all about this book when I tuck you in tonight."

"Deal!" She slipped into the chair, grabbed a paper towel for a disposable plate and breathed deeply. "This is like the best night ever."

Clearly, she didn't have to deal with the reporters outside or the constant requests for interviews. The number had actually risen today, and he knew he couldn't take the kids back to his house for the night, but he hadn't wanted Christa to face this new situation alone. Not with so much on the line. The boys' well-being, and hers. To unexpectedly become a parent to two grieving children wasn't a walk in the park. He understood that better than most. Once the kids had eaten, he'd slip them out the back door and into Renzo's car parked on the next block. Parking an unfamiliar car over there had offered him the chance to be here and offer his support, and to slip out quietly once dinner was over.

He reached for Vangie's hand to say grace. She took his hand and reached for Christa's on the other side, and when Nathan grabbed hold of the pretty teacher's left hand, he couldn't help but notice they made a nice circle.

He started to give thanks as one of the little guys began crying upstairs.

Five pairs of eyes looked up, partly because it was new, but mostly because the tragic sobs weren't just the usual sounds of a fussy little kid.

This was sorrow and heartbreak mixed with grief and mourning.

Christa stood quickly. "Sorry." She released the kids' hands and slipped out around Nathan. "I've got to go to him."

She went up the stairs quickly, but it was long minutes before the sobs diminished.

Vangie and Nathan exchanged looks. Were they thinking about losing their mom?

Nathan barely remembered Hadley. The unfairness of that always hit Tug crosswise because the woman who gave him life should at least be a memory. Shouldn't she?

"It's hard to lose your mom." Evangeline picked up a piece of pizza, then set it down again. "It just makes everything different, doesn't it? Like forever? And it never gets to be the same again."

Glenn brought over a pitcher of lemonade. "Things don't stay the same regardless, do they?"

Evangeline looked up at him, puzzled.

"Even when folks stay here on earth, things change. People get sick. People move. They get new jobs or new houses or new families. Because for everything on this planet, every little thing and big thing, there is a season, Vangie. Good seasons and not-so-good seasons. But the seasons come and go just like they've always done, and we move on."

"To a new season," she told him. Not in her usual excited voice, but in a more subdued tone. "Like now. Like fall."

"Yes." Glenn settled into the seat next to her, the one Christa had vacated. "The things of fall are for the fall. Not the spring. Same with summer and winter, so our job is to work with the seasons. With the times. Do our best and trust God to take care of us."

"But God didn't take care of the little boys' mother." Vangie whispered the words. She glanced at the stairs, where the sobs had diminished. "Or my mom. So maybe He can't do all the stuff people ask Him to do. Because if He could, why wouldn't He save all the moms? Especially when kids need them?"

His dad could have sloughed off the answer onto Tug's shoulders.

He didn't. He chewed a bite of pizza thoughtfully, then aimed a look at Vangie. "Things happen all the time, precious girl. Things I can't explain. I can't tell you why your mom got sick and why she didn't get better. It's as much a mystery to me now as it was then. And I can't explain whatever happened to the boys' mother..." He sat back in his chair, still thoughtful. "But I know this. That God gave Grandma and me two amazing grandchildren to help raise. A wonderful opportunity for us to help your dad, and for you to be a help to your grandma. So maybe having a family in place is what God wants in case things happen."

"Like to be smart and be nice to each other?" Nathan seemed to grasp the idea despite his young age. "So when people need help, we can give it to them."

"Just like that."

Nathan looked satisfied.

Not Vangie. And when the little guy upstairs began crying again, she blinked twice. Not in surprise. But to hold back tears. She knew what the boy was feeling. She'd lived it. And the emotion on her tender face right now showed him she hadn't forgotten it, and that realization made him think maybe not remembering wasn't such a bad gig, after all.

Christa debated taking a day off from work. Maybe two. The school would grant her bereavement days, but what would she do with them? What could she get done while Marta's death was under investigation?

"You're worried." Darla Moyer slid a cup of coffee across the counter toward Christa the next morning. "And I don't expect you slept a lot."

"True on both counts." Christa picked up the coffee, then set it right back down. "I should stay home with them today, shouldn't I? Nurture them. Help them to feel safe again."

"You sure can," Darla agreed. She hooked her foot around a chair rung and slid it out from the table so she could take a seat. "But you might want to save that time off for a week or two. Totally up to you. I know the school won't care, the days are in your contract, but right now everything's in flux, so maybe staying on the quiet side of normal is a good thing. The boys can hang out here. We'll play games and be silly and eat apple slices and peanut butter. Sometimes the simplest answers are the best."

"I see that in school all the time." Christa breathed deeply. "You don't mind? I can come straight back when school's dismissed."

Darla held her mug of coffee with both hands. She studied the mug, then Christa. "Whatever these two have been through has been at least traumatic. And maybe even horrific. For now, I'd say we keep things nice and easy, and let them readjust to a normal life through regular situations. We can give time a chance to do what time does best. Heal their wounds."

It made sense. And it was the kind of common sense her mother used to offer, so why didn't she listen back then?

"And don't feel guilty for making the sensible decision," Darla added. "There is plenty of guilt to go around when you're raising kids, so let's start you off on the right side of that. Shrug it off and get on with life. I'm fine with whatever decision you make, Christa." She raised her gaze toward the nearby stairway. "They're not the only ones whose lives just got a thorough shake-up."

How kind of Tug's mother to recognize that. It made her feel less guilty about being a little overwhelmed. "I'll go in. You're sure you didn't have anything going on today? Because I'm pretty sure you did."

"I volunteer at the homeless shelter in Quincy. I make food for lunch and help prep for dinner two days a week, but my sister Grace is taking my shifts. She bartered with me." A quick smile—the one she'd gifted genetically to her son—brightened her face. "If she can have unlimited time with the boys, she'll help in the shelter as needed. Her kids are both single and professionally driven, so no grandkids as yet. Which means Jeremy and Jonah will be basking in the love of two funny grandma-types."

"Thank you so much." Christa wasn't a random hugger. There hadn't been all that many people to hug in her life, but she hugged Darla right now. "I don't know how or why this all happened, or how your family wandered into my life at the most opportune moment, but I'm so grateful for the understanding and the help. I bet you were a great foster mom."

"Well, thank you right back." Darla returned the hug from her seat. "Now I'm going to enjoy this coffee and a quiet kitchen until the boys wake up. Then I'll hit the ground running. Nothing better to keep us grandmas in shape than chasing around after little ones."

Christa tiptoed up the stairs. The boys were still asleep when she finished getting ready. They'd wanted to share a bed. Understandable, when life had torn so much apart. Jonah was on the inside of the bed, blocked from falling by the wall, and Jeremy was tucked in beside him, as if sleep didn't stop Jeremy from protecting his little brother. Darla had installed some kind of guardrail to keep him from falling out.

Smart. And handy. Christa didn't even know such things existed. *And how much more don't you know? What makes you think you can raise two boys who've probably seen nothing but trouble all their days?*

She didn't let the mental warning jar her.

She could either allow worry to consume her, or use her rough past to help ease the boys into a new normal.

She went downstairs barefoot and slipped her sandals on when she got into the kitchen. "I didn't want to wake them," she told Darla. "If things go badly, call me, okay?"

"I will. And Jubilee is stopping by later to go over some things, so she'll probably be here when you get home."

It wasn't home.

Christa knew that.

But it felt like the kind of home she'd always dreamed of.

For now, the boys were safe and beloved, and she had the blessing of a good job. A job she'd worked hard to get, a position she loved. That had been her mother's dream, to see both girls successful, only Margaretta had never seen her daughter's success. She'd lived through Christa's failures, then passed away. If there was a way to see things from Heaven...

Christa glanced up as she moved to her car. The clutch of reporters had left to go to the school, hoping to catch Tug there, no doubt.

Could her mother see what was happening here? Would it make her happy or sad?

She pulled into the school lot a few minutes later. Tug was talking to reporters again. She couldn't hear what he was saying, but she heard laughter and could make out the smiles on the journalists' faces.

He made people laugh.

He kept people safe.

And he made them feel better about things.

Friends on social media had been raving about the newest superhero movie to hit theaters and break all kinds of box-office records.

The action-packed movies were fun and entertaining, but they were fiction. At the moment, she was pretty sure the real deal was the guy with the engaging smile out front.

She walked into the school, thinking that reality was way better than fiction sometimes.

Evangeline was coming down the hall. She spotted Christa and her face lit up. "Ms. Alero, you will never ever in a million years guess what happened!"

"That being the case, you should simply tell me ASAP, thereby sparing me a million years of useless questioning."

Evangeline burst out laughing and grabbed her hand. "I think I might have gotten my dad a date. Maybe two dates!" Excitement hiked the girl's tone. "And the TV station wants him to come and meet them on their show! Wouldn't that be so much fun?"

First of all, who was talking to this eight-year-old about dates for her dad?

And second, airing your life on-air wouldn't be the least bit fun, Christa thought, but it wasn't her job to rain on the girl's parade. "It could be, they have TV shows that do surprise dates, but I wouldn't have thought your dad would be into that."

"My dad is the best," affirmed the third grader, "but he doesn't always know what's best for him, you know?"

Christa was not about to go down that rabbit hole with the man's daughter. "He is the adult. Correct?"

Evangeline nodded vigorously as they neared the classroom. "Exactly. That's why he needs someone else to do things with. He does everything with me and Nathan. I heard Grandma say that kind of stifles other options. That means he doesn't get a lot of choices," she explained in a frank voice.

Yup. Boss in training.

Christa bit back a smile and kept her tone serious. "I know a lot of children who would love that kind of attention."

"We do." Vangie stopped, but she didn't let go of Christa's hand, and when she said the next words, she worked her way further into Christa's heart. "He loves us so much. He tucks us in every single night. He says our prayers with us. Then he kisses Nathan good-night. Then me. And then—" her tone hitched slightly "—he gets up and walks away. Down the hall. Just him. I hear his footsteps, Ms. Alero, and they're always alone. So sometimes I wish he had someone else to talk to. To be with. To laugh with. Instead of being all alone every single night."

Vangie's compassion didn't just grab Christa's heart. It wrenched it open. She wasn't just trying to set her dad up for dates.

The precocious child was trying to set him up for a

joyful life. The unselfishness of Evangeline's ploy made Christa realize the girl had gotten more than the killer smile and good looks from her father.

She inherited his passion to make things right in the world. To fix things. To look out for others. What a wonderful combination it was. "You've got a loving and giving heart, Evangeline Moyer."

"Well, thank you." Vangie moved toward her desk, musing. "Now I just have to figure out the long division I've been practicing with Dad at home, memorize the states and get Dad on a date. Maybe even by this weekend."

Tug had called Vangie an overachiever.

He was correct, but Christa hoped he saw the reasoning behind her actions.

All she really wanted was for her daddy to not be alone.

Chapter Five

The local TV station wanted to do an on-air introduction between Tug and a single nurse who worked at Central Washington Hospital. They'd emailed him a time frame and a picture of the very pretty woman, and let him know the whole thing would be paid in full by a local car dealership whose tagline was "Have We Got a Match for You!"

Evangeline thought it was amazingly romantic.

Maybe it was by an eight-year-old's standards. Thirty extra years changed that perspective.

He refused the offer graciously, citing the campaign, time restrictions and a conflict of interest because the family that owned the dealership were contributing supporters of his campaign. That wouldn't look right to anyone and he knew his opponent would be watching closely, so why give him ammunition?

Tug slipped into the middle school halfway between lunch and dismissal.

This was the "dead" time in schools. The most rigorous and weighted courses were the morning focus at

Golden Grove Middle School, following the premise that kids learned better before lunch, but that left the afternoon more lax.

He saw a few kids hanging around a side hallway. They scattered as soon as they spotted him.

Bad sign.

He moved their way. Called to them in a soft voice. One stopped.

The others ducked into classrooms.

He motioned to the girl who'd stopped to wait, then followed his instincts into the boys' bathroom.

The smell of weed smoke hit him when he opened the door. The bathroom was empty. Time was short, because the buses would arrive in less than ninety minutes.

He keyed his radio and called Renzo for backup. His first instinct was to call for a search. Courts had ruled that suspicion of drug use wasn't enough cause for a full school search, but that wasn't why he scratched the idea. For the moment, he wanted those boys to think they'd gotten away with something. Once they thought they had the upper hand, he'd go for the jugular.

The principal wouldn't like it. She'd throw a fuss, but if they were going to solve this school's problems before they grew worse, they needed to jump on this. Better to have the kids understand expectations in September than be surprised by a school-wide search in November.

He didn't take the seventh-grade girl to his office. No way was he going to interview a kid without witnesses. He escorted her to the main office, sat her in a chair, then squatted in front of her.

She looked scared.

Good. She should be afraid. Kids that smoked pot or dealt drugs should fear cops because they were breaking the law. On purpose.

"What's your name?"

She stared at him, then turned her face away.

"I can tell you her name," cut in the assistant principal. "It's—"

"I'd prefer to hear it from her," Tug told the woman. "But thank you."

The girl set her jaw hard.

Tug pretended he didn't have a care in the world. He slid out a chair from alongside the assistant principal's desk and took a seat. "I've got all day," he assured the girl and he used his most nonchalant voice. "My kids can take the bus, there's someone there to watch them, and it wouldn't be the first time I've had to stay all night on a job. Don't expect it will be the last, either." He settled back, stretched, then yawned. The stretch was for effect. The yawn was quite real. Thoughts of Christa and those two orphaned boys had interrupted his sleep the night before.

"You can't keep me here all night." The girl's eyes widened in indignation, then narrowed. "You're just trying to scare me. Like they do on cop shows. I'm not scared." False bravado darkened her expression. "When those buses come, you have to let me get on."

Tug held her gaze for a few long beats, then quirked his jaw. "Wrong answer. First, it would be easier to talk to you here, rather than at the station, but that can be arranged." He paused as another deputy sheriff came into the room. "Renzo, thanks for coming right over."

"No problem." Lorenzo Calloway didn't sit. He folded

his arms across his chest and loomed. Also on purpose. "Drugs in schools bring me on the run. We taking her in?"

"That's up to her." Tug hunched forward. "We can do that or just call her parents to come hear what she has to say."

Her face paled.

She darted a glance around as if looking for help. The assistant principal surprised Tug by saying, "Tillie, you know you don't do the things they're talking about. Tell them who you are and what you know."

"And get beat on by my brother tonight? I don't think so." The girl—Tillie—made a face and shook her head. "You know Hayward, Miss Spencer. If he ever had a nice bone in his body, it's long gone."

"Your brother hits you?" Tug kept his voice deliberately soft. "I'm sorry, Tillie."

"So now you're going to go all nice on me because you think I'm a poor kid who doesn't know better. I know better, and Miss Spencer is right. I don't do any of the stuff those boys are into, but if I don't play by my brother's rules, someone gets hurt, and that someone is usually me. And I don't like getting hurt."

That was a game changer.

Tug couldn't send the girl into a situation where she might get beaten up by her brother. "Listen." He reached into his pocket and gave her his card. "I hear you. I don't want you to get hurt, either, and I want to say thank you to you for stopping when I told you to. You did the right thing."

"When school's over, the right thing often turns out to be the stupidest thing because those boys are going to tell Hayward," she told him in a frank voice. "He'll know by suppertime, and if I'm very lucky, he might be too wasted to do anything about it."

"Do you want to go into foster care, Tillie?" The assistant principal's face stayed compassionate as she asked a very difficult question.

"No, ma'am. That would just about kill my mama. My little brother needs someone around to make sure he's taken care of after school. He's got me and I've got him."

With a miserable older brother running the show. Tug handed her the card. "Are your mom and dad around at all?"

The question made her squirm, or maybe it was how to phrase the answer that unnerved her. Finally she said, "There's no dad. Mom works at the nursing home. But she has the afternoon shift. That's the only one they had open when she got to be a nurse last year."

Tug read her expression. She was caught in a tough spot. Hardworking mother, no father, an older brother on the road to nowhere good and a little brother. "All right, Tillie. I won't say anything more, and don't take the card home. Memorize my number. Leave the card at school. I don't want your brother finding it, okay?"

She held his gaze, then nodded. Her expression softened. "Thank you." She stood, started for the door, then stopped. "Tillie Anderson." She looked over her shoulder at Tug. "That's my name, sir. Tillie Anderson."

"It's nice to meet you, Tillie."

Her wince indicated it might not have been all that nice for her to meet him, but she went back to class.

Tug spoke with the assistant principal, left a message

for the principal, thanked Renzo for a quick backup, then went over to the elementary school, a few hundred yards away.

He paused by Nathan's classroom door. Peeked in. The first-grade class was thoroughly engaged in a story. Twenty-three kids, so young and innocent. In a few years, Vangie would be attending the middle school. Then the high school. Nathan would soon follow. Which meant he needed to do whatever he could to fix the troubled school now.

His phone buzzed.

It was a call from that local reporter, the one he'd spoken to yesterday morning, requesting an interview in place of the on-air date.

Aunt Grace's words came back to him. *This could help spread your teen ministry.*

Was it right for him to capitalize on something Vangie shouldn't have done? Or was he foolish not to jump on board because he could use his fifteen minutes of fame to reach more teens?

He took the call, agreed to an after-school interview at his home, then hung up the phone. When the buses had pulled out of the drive, he brought Nathan over to Christa's room to pick up Evangeline. "Any calls from the home front?" he asked Christa when he came in the door.

Bemused, she nodded. That cute worry line reformed, and the urge to smooth it away didn't seem quite so surprising today. "Not from, but to. I called your mom three times, which makes me a nervous new surrogate mother who probably knows next to nothing about caring for little boys and my ineptitude is showing."

"I'd go with caring and concerned," he corrected her. He smiled at her, and when she glanced up, she held his gaze.

He wanted to keep on smiling like this. Just like this. "My mom's worked with new parents before. She knows the drill. And I don't think there's such a thing as too much caring, is there?"

"Can we go to Grandma's and see the boys?" Vangie pleaded. "I can play with them and we can get my ponies and stuff out of the attic."

"Mom kept some old toys in storage in case they did foster care again," he explained to Christa. To Vangie, he said, "We're not going to Grandma's. We're meeting with a reporter to talk about your video."

"For real?" she squealed. "About the lady they want you to date?" She stopped packing her always-laden backpack and tossed her hands in the air, deliberately dramatic. "Dad, I am so proud of you right now!"

He rolled his eyes. "No date. Stop trying to run my life, Vangie."

She frowned, but it wasn't a full-on frown. More like a biding-her-time expression.

He tapped his watch. "We've got to be there in twenty minutes, and that will probably spur another round of interest in my love life, but it will give me a chance to talk on-air about kids with problems. Which is the only reason I'm doing this," he told his daughter. "Nathan, you ready, buddy?"

"Yup, and I get to see my friend CeeCee this weekend, because we're living in her old house. That will be so much fun!"

CeeCee was Libby Creighton-McClaren's daughter. She and Nathan shared a love for growing things. Nathan had inherited the Moyer farming gene.

Not Tug. He'd become a cop , leaving no one to take over the Moyer family farm. When Hadley passed away, his parents had sold the farm so they would have more time to help him with the kids.

The kids headed toward the door.

He turned to follow them, but not before Christa saw his expression. "Is seeing that little girl a bad thing?" she asked softly.

"No, it's fine." He let the kids get a little bit farther ahead before he said more. "She's a great kid, but I just realized we're in the heart of apple season and this weekend will be crazy busy at the O'Laughlin barn up the road. A barn my father sold to them. If we're staying in their house, there's no way to keep folks from realizing it on a big apple weekend because they park right outside the old house."

"That's a problem, all right, but maybe one with an obvious solution," she told him. "Maybe your kids would just like to go home. To their own house. Home is always best, isn't it? Face the dragons and send them on their way?"

She was right.

Maybe by giving this reporter a quick exclusive, the rest of the pack would go away. "You're right. I'll move home this weekend and get things back to normal."

"A kind family, a decent home, clothes to wear and food on the table. The best kind of normal there is," she agreed. She slung her bag over her shoulder and walked down the hall with him, and it wasn't her expression that set him wondering.

It was the poignancy in her voice. The hint of longing, as if the simple normal she'd described didn't exist.

It didn't for Tillie. It didn't for a lot of the kids who messaged him and shared his stuff online. But hearing that wistful note in her voice made him want to make it her reality. "You appreciate the everyday things we tend to take for granted."

"Yes." Her quick smile was his reward. "Why yearn for riches when enough is as good as a feast?"

"You guys are kinda slow." Nathan and Vangie had already reached the door. Miss Ivy had gone home, and there was no longer a bank of reporters at the school's edge. Tug was real glad to see that.

He reached out and pushed the door open, then held it for Christa and the kids to walk through. When Nathan tried to do the same with the outer door, Tug had to hold himself back from intervening. The heavy door wasn't cooperating, and when the little guy finally had it open and tucked behind his back, Tug high-fived him. "Thank you, my man."

Nathan beamed up at him, the gaping spot of two missing teeth a reminder that time was marching on. Nathan was still getting baby teeth when he had lost his mother. He was growing by leaps and bounds these days.

"Can we go to Grandma's for supper, Dad? After we talk with the lady? I really want to see the little boys again. We barely saw them yesterday."

"When things are back to normal you'll be going to

Grandma's every day again, which means you'll see Jeremy and Jonah regularly."

"It *is* pasta night." Nathan didn't beg. He never begged, but he was quite adept at pointing out the obvious. They all loved Glenn Moyer's red sauce and pasta. Nathan shrugged his little shoulders as he began climbing into Tug's SUV.

"Although your grandma might have been too busy with the little guys to make dinner tonight," said Christa.

Nathan, Vangie and Tug exchanged grins. "Mom's great at baking, but when it comes to cooking, that's Dad's wheelhouse. He starts his sauce early in the day and it's like a work of art. Sausage, meatballs, pork."

"Vegetarian special, hmm?" Christa mused.

Tug scrubbed a hand to the back of his neck. "There are two kinds of Westerners in Central Washington, ma'am."

He'd hoped the *ma'am* would make her smile again, like it did yesterday.

Success!

"The real ones who like or grow meat as a regular part of their daily diet—"

"I did notice that lots of people who don't even have farms or acreage seem to have a cow or a pig or something penned up in their yard. So that's the norm?" she asked.

"There's been a fair amount of people who have come in from other areas that don't quite get it," he admitted. "Some folks think the whole world should be one big fruit orchard, and their ideas don't jibe with the true locals. I like apples real well," he finished with a wink. "Alongside a nice steak or some barbecued chicken."

"Dad, we have to hurry." Vangie tapped a nonexistent watch on her slim wrist. "You don't want to be late."

"Shall I tell your mom you're coming by, then?" Christa asked as she crossed to her parking spot.

How could he say no? Nathan loved his grandpa's sauce and the kid could pack away an amazing amount of rigatoni, another thing he had in common with his grandpa. "Yes. Thank you."

"Will do." She tucked her bag into the back seat and climbed into the worn black hatchback, a car that had seen better days a long time ago. Not exactly the best choice for a Central Washington winter with two kids. He waited until the car started and she'd pulled away before he headed to the old O'Laughlin house.

He parked behind the new barn Libby had built after a storm took their old one down. He was ushering the kids to the house when the reporter drove in and followed his directions by pulling around back.

She and her cameraman followed them in.

He'd dreaded this interview since saying yes, but thirty minutes later, it was done, it hadn't been bad at all, and she'd given him time to talk about why he already had an online presence for Vangie to access, a perfect segue into talking about his *Fire Within* ministry.

Once the crew left, he got the kids into the car and swung around his end of town to scope things out.

No one was there. The bevy of news trucks hadn't just dissipated. It had disappeared completely.

He breathed an audible sigh of relief.

But there—

On his side porch—

Were packages. A pile of packages.

Except he'd ordered nothing in days, so why were there packages on his porch? He went instantly to total cop brain.

Bombs.

Poisons.

Hate mail.

He kept driving to his parents' place, sent the kids inside and called the station house once he couldn't be overheard. He couldn't risk there being something weird or dangerous in the packages. How would Nathan and Vangie ever feel safe in their home again if someone was targeting them?

He'd lie low over here and let the professionals handle it. Then he called the local postmaster at home and had her hold all of his mail and packages there. He hung up the phone, drew a breath and walked inside.

A counter full of cookies, brownies and cakes awaited him. "Is the church having a bake sale?" he asked as he grabbed street clothes from a stash he kept at his mother's. Normally he wouldn't wear his uniform home, but the sheriff had given him permission to wear it during the interview.

"Gifts," replied his mother as she chopped canned peaches into baby-sized bites for Jonah. "From women who want to take care of you and the kids."

He came to a standstill. Stared at her. Then the stacks of baked goods. Then her again. "You cannot be serious."

"Just wait until you see the mail sack in the dining

room," she added cheerfully. "Your popularity suddenly knows no bounds," she went on, not even trying to disguise her grin. "The power of social media and the US postal service."

Unbelievable.

The food. The mail. And as he walked through the living room, Christa came toward him, holding Jeremy.

The boy reached out instantly. "Hey! Hey! Copper Guy!" He catapulted himself into Tug's arms and held on for dear life, and as those little arms grabbed tight around Tug's neck, and he spotted the look of sweet compassion on Christa's face, the last thing he wanted to do was let go. And for a fleeting second, as he gazed into Christa's big brown eyes, he wondered why he should. But he knew why, better than most. He'd dropped the ball once and wrecked the beautiful dream he'd called family.

No way was he going to take that chance again.

Chapter Six

Jeremy had fallen for the sheriff's deputy. Big-time.

Based on the outpouring from women across the country—and a few international entries, according to Tug's mother—falling for Tug Moyer wasn't all that difficult. It was a good thing to recognize while remembering that he was off-limits. Totally. If Tug Moyer was a superhero, she was his kryptonite, and she didn't need that on her conscience along with everything else.

But the little guy's obvious affection was good to see.

"Despite all the packages, letters and baked goods, I think your number one fan is right here. In your arms." She said the words just loud enough for Tug to hear. "You saved his life. Somehow he knows that. Nothing like the faith of a child, is there?"

"There's not."

"I'm glad you decided to come over tonight," she continued as the boy snuggled into Tug's shoulder. "He recognizes you as a friend. A hero." And when Tug started to dismiss that, she raised a hand. "You're going to say you were just doing your job, but he understands somehow that your job kept him and his baby brother safe. So it's good for him to see you."

"And I like seeing him, too." Tug pulled the little guy back far enough to make eye contact, then tipped him halfway over. "That way I can tip him upside down!"

"Eek!"

For a brief moment, Christa wasn't sure if Jeremy was going to laugh or cry, or if she should jump in to save him, so when he giggled out loud and Tug did it again, she breathed easier. "If you're okay with him, I'm going to get Jonah so we can feed him. And since I've never in my life fed a baby of any sort, I'm still in watch-and-learn mode."

"Never?" Tug sounded surprised as she moved toward the porch.

"No siblings. Marta was the only other relative we had in America and she came north a long time ago."

"But neighbors? Friends with little brothers or sisters? Folks from church?"

She kept her face serene with effort. "None of those applied. I grew up in a tough neighborhood. Not much camaraderie."

Sympathy smoothed the laugh wrinkles around his eyes. "That couldn't have been fun."

His sympathy drew her, but she wasn't into high-risk romance. She'd come here to create a whole new life. She'd pictured it as her and Marta, working together, *familia*. Now it was just her and the boys, and there was no way she could allow a doomed romance to lead her astray.

Glenn Moyer met her at the front door. He was holding Jonah. He spotted her and gave her a thumbs-up.

"Swap. You get the cute little guy and I go start the pasta."

"Deal," she told him, and when the older Moyer passed Tug and Jeremy, he didn't just walk by. He paused and gave the little guy a head bump, real gentle. The kind of thing fictional dads did on TV commercials, and the image of the two big men and the little boy engraved itself on her brain.

Perfect.

Jonah didn't give her time to dwell on it.

He wriggled in her arms and pointed to the floor. "Down."

"Uh-uh. Food first. Then down."

He looked like he was going to protest until she turned the corner into the kitchen and he spotted a high chair with food. "Me! Me! Me!"

Darla drew the chair back from the table so Christa could set him down, and the moment he was in the chair, not even strapped in yet, his little hands grabbed at the food.

Seeing his hunger and his instant instinctive reaction, Christa swallowed hard.

She understood that reaction.

She'd known hunger as a child. Not starvation, since there were always soup kitchens to go to, but they didn't always fit into Margaretta's work schedule.

Yeah, she knew hunger, and that gnawing feeling of emptiness inside.

Tug came up alongside her.

She glanced up.

Big mistake, because he was studying her with the kind of look that made her want to draw close, or maybe be drawn close *by him*, tucked into the curve of his arm. If his expression was an invitation, she was pretty sure that hers was an answering acceptance.

He shifted gears. On purpose, it seemed. And while that was the sensible choice, it didn't make her stop longing for the sweet moment they'd just shared. "Mom, what are we going to do with all of these baked goods?"

"If you guys could load them into the car, we can drive them over to the food pantry in Quincy tomorrow morning."

"Nathan, you up for helping your dad and me move this stuff to the car so we can donate it?" Glenn asked as he set a kettle of water on the stove, then switched the back burner to high. "I expect we can get it done by the time the pasta's ready."

"All the stuff?" Nathan turned a glum look at the stacks of plastic containers. Some had ribbons. Some had bows. Some came with letters attached. "Can't we keep some of it? Like the really good stuff?"

"We'll see." Darla filled Jonah's plastic plate again. "We can always bake things, honey. I love doing that with you guys. The folks who get things at the food pantry don't have that option. Some of them don't have stoves and some don't even have homes. I say let's be as generous as we can be. Okay?"

"Like they don't have a place to go?" Nathan hadn't gotten his father's reddish-brown eyes, but he'd gotten his big heart. It was there in the look of surprise he aimed at his grandmother. "Not a house or anyplace?"

"For some, yes. They don't have a house or anyplace," Darla confirmed. "These cookies and cakes will be a real blessing to them."

Nathan grabbed a container from the overladen countertop. "Then we should take them some all the time, Grandma. Like not just now," he persisted with a six-year-old's logic. "Every single day because we always have cookies. And you make the best!"

"Out of the mouths of babes." Tug palmed the boy's head, then went to settle Jeremy into a seat.

Jeremy had other ideas. "No." He gripped tight to Tug's neck. "I stay with you." He sent a very firm look up to Tug.

Tug held the boy's gaze. Then he winked. "All right. You can be part of the Feed the Homeless Committee, my man."

Jeremy didn't have a clue what Tug meant, but he knew he got to stay safe in his hero's arms. He aimed the biggest, brightest smile up at Tug, and when Tug leaned forward and kissed the little boy's forehead, Christa's heart fluttered again.

There was something sweet and engaging about the exchange, which was probably why romantic TV movies paired swoon-worthy guys with little kids all the time. The whole image had her thinking about things like happily-ever-afters, which meant she had to put more effort into blocking impossible thoughts and rogue ideas.

"More?" Jonah peered up at her and Darla as the guys began loading the cartons and tubs and even the occasional shoebox of treats. "More?"

Darla handed him some cheesy crackers and a little chopped chicken, then poured herself and Christa a mug of coffee. "You're lost in thought," she noted as she set the mugs down. The guys trooped in for another load. Then back out. And when they were out of hearing, Christa answered.

"When I was little, Marta would share her stuff with me," she told her. "All her stuff." She watched as Jonah picked between the bits of meat to snag the little crackers. It wasn't until he chewed the last cracker that he gave the bites of meat a chance. "If she got a treat in school, she brought it home to me. If she had candy from a neighbor, she shared half with me. Back then she always thought of others first.

"But all that changed when she got to be a teenager," she continued. "Suddenly she focused on what she had and what she couldn't have, and she wasn't afraid to break the law to get what she wanted. It was a complete turnaround. That's why my mother gave her an ultimatum, which I didn't understand when I was twelve. My mother said Marta was becoming a bad influence on me, and that she had to straighten up or leave the house. So she moved out after a huge fight and a lot of angry words between them. I was so mad. Mad that she was gone, mad that I was alone so much of the time and mad that we had nothing." She sighed softly. "I became a trial to my mother, and no matter how well I do now, I still feel the guilt of how I behaved back then."

"'When I was a child...'" Darla began quoting Paul's poignant words to the people of Corinth.

"I love that verse," Christa admitted. "And I believe it, but it doesn't soften the guilt for being a first-class jerk to the one person who loved me more than anything."

"Is your mother alive?"

"No." She drew another breath, a firmer one this

time. "She died before I finished my undergrad degree. Before I became a teacher. But I like to think that she can see what I've done. What I've become. She'd be pleased after years of so much worry."

"She'd be proud of her beautiful daughter," Darla agreed. "So how did you reconnect with Marta?"

"She found me on the internet and sent letters a few years ago. I was a long-term substitute teacher in a sub-urban California district. She sounded good. She told me about her life up here, how beautiful it was. How she was working in housekeeping at the hospital and build-ing a new life." She got quiet as the men came through again. When they'd taken the last stack of containers to the SUV, she faced Darla. "How do things go from that to this so quickly? Two hungry, neglected little boys." She gripped the back of the chair tightly because it made no sense. None at all.

"The lure of drugs overshadows a lot."

"It must. But I don't get it, Darla." Christa whis-pered the words as the toddler worked to get sticky fin-gers around slippery bits of food. "A choice that leaves children in danger? I don't think I can ever understand that."

"And yet here you are, at just the right time. A new job in the very same county that oversees the boys' wel-fare. I don't think that was coincidence, Christa. Maybe somehow Marta knew you were coming. Maybe she got your letters. Or maybe God's timing brought you here when you would be most needed. You wanted to reconnect with family. And you did, but in an unex-pected way."

Christa refilled Jonah's sippy cup and set it on the

table. "A part of me longs for normal." She watched the boy grasp the two-handled cup and draw on the top with amazing gusto for such a small person. "I don't care about some big American dream. I just want the everyday goodness and kindness you see on TV and in magazines. When you come from so little, everything grows in magnitude."

"Wise words." Darla patted her hand. Jonah must have found their serious conversation boring, because he smacked his cup down and offered the two women a most delightful grin.

"Down! Down! Down!"

"After a good washup, my man," Darla told him. She reached for him, but Christa intervened.

"I'll scrub him up. I've got to get good at all this and I watched you at the sink, although I am amazed at how quickly he moves and how adeptly he avoids the wash-cloth," she added a minute later, when the little one kept ducking his head.

Tug came in. The minute he spotted the struggle for cleanliness, he moistened a second washcloth and sprang into action. "This means war!"

He brandished the washcloth like a cowboy with a lariat, and when the little guy burst out laughing at his antics, Tug swooped in with a gentle but clean sweep of one side of the toddler's face. "Almost there!" He acted ridiculous again, and when Jonah started giggling help-lessly, Tug swept in and swiped the cloth gently over the opposite side of his rounded cheeks.

"But how do we do the hands while he's sitting?" asked Christa, and Tug's answer made perfect sense.

"That would be a fruitless gesture," he told her.

"Bring him over here. We can wash them right under the faucet. It removes any possible ammunition on his part and the hands don't stay sticky."

She slipped Jonah out of the chair, then kept him out-turned to save her shirt from the onslaught of dropped food. Tug had turned the water on. Warm, not hot. Not cold. While she held the boy in her arms, Tug drew his tiny hands beneath the stream of water.

The toddler declared an instant ceasefire.

He stopped squirming, enthralled by the feel of warm water. He splashed his hands, clapped them, then laughed when water spattered all three of them, but within seconds his little fingers were washed clean.

Tug turned the water off.

He lifted a hand towel and wiped the boy's hands, then face, and then—

He reached out and gently passed the soft cotton towel across Christa's cheek. First one. Then the other. And he held her gaze while doing it, as if he couldn't stop holding her gaze.

Danger zone.

She knew it.

He didn't. Or maybe he did, but he didn't realize how real the danger zone could be to his life. His career.

She needed to squash the attraction right now, but when he took the towel and tapped her nose with it, his grin wiped rational thought away. "The kid's got a wicked splash pattern. Now you're both good to go. Dad?" He stepped away as if totally unaffected by the last thirty seconds while her heart tripped into race-pace mode. "Water's boiling."

"I'm on it." Glenn came in with Nathan and Jeremy.

Tug's phone rang right then. He answered it, and his expression went from concern to chagrin in quick motion. "Cookies? Cakes? And photographs?"

She couldn't hear the other end of the conversation, but when Tug rubbed a hand to the back of his neck, she got the gist. "Dad and I will gather them up and donate them. Thanks, Bill, and, yes, I will expect the entire station house to haze me for the foreseeable future. Thank you all for saving us from such dangerous baked goods."

With Jeremy's hand tucked firmly into his, Nathan was leading the younger boy into the front room. "Dad, can I show Jeremy how my race cars work? I think he'll like really, really like them."

"Sure. But don't leave a mess for Grandma to pick up, okay?" He shifted his focus to Glenn as he stirred the rapidly boiling pasta. "Dad, you sure you don't mind dropping that stuff off in Quincy in the morning?"

"Shall I grab whatever they found at your house, too?" His father's droll tone said he'd eavesdropped on his son's phone conversation.

Tug sent him a rueful grin of acknowledgment. "Yes, thank you. I saw a pile of boxes on the side porch and went into cop mode, which means the bomb squad just rescued our family from cookies, cakes and nut breads."

"How can you guarantee that the food is safe?" asked Christa. "The food shelves where I grew up would only take things purchased in grocery stores. Or commercial shops."

"We're in a pretty down-to-earth part of the state," Tug replied. "I can't be totally sure they'll take this stuff, but we're a little looser out here than in the city."

"Although you did call out the bomb squad," noted Christa.

Her quick comeback made him smile. "I did. And I'll never hear the end of it, so that just makes the week even more special. My interview on the local news airs tomorrow morning, so that should make things interesting all over again. But then—*maybe*—peace. That's the hope."

He didn't overreact.

She loved that. Her early life had been rife with over-reactions, except at school. School had been her safety net. She'd been blessed with a great memory and good teachers, so even when things grew bad at home—as the neighborhood spiraled downhill and the lure of belonging pulled her into bad decisions—she was on safe, steady ground at school. In the end, being a good student and a hard worker had pulled her out of the decay and into a new light. She just wished it hadn't taken her so long.

Jonah started heading back to the table. She intercepted him before he could get messy again and scooped him up. "Let's get you into jammies, little man."

"And I'll clean this up." Tug took the dishcloth over to the table. When she came back down a few minutes later, the table was set for four, and Tug, Nathan and Evangeline were gone.

Disappointment hit her squarely.

The house seemed emptier without them. She tried to hide her reaction, but she was pretty sure not much got past Tug's mother.

"Tug took food to go," Darla explained when Christa

came into the room. "He wanted to get the kids settled after supper, and it's already getting late."

"I'm new with raising kids, but I know it's important to keep schoolkids on some sort of schedule so they can be at their best each day." She called Jeremy to the table while Jonah busied himself with pots and pans from the lowest cupboard. And when Darla handed the toddler a short wooden spoon, the boy became a full-on percussionist on the kitchen floor.

They had pasta with fresh red sauce and a toddler's musical accompaniment, and as they ate and talked, Christa's concerns lessened.

She'd thought being with Tug's family would be horribly awkward.

But their humor and commonsense natures made sure it wasn't, and when the boys were finally tucked into bed, Christa sank onto the couch and locked eyes with Tug's mother. "I have newfound respect for working moms, and single parents get an extra round of applause. This isn't a game for amateurs," she told Darla and Glenn. "First, hats off to your son for managing as well as he does, and second, please feel free to give me all the advice you can because I still have two hours of school prep work to do and I'm beat."

"Oh, I hear you." Compassion laced Darla's tone. "First advice. Make the best use of your in-school time to get prep work and grading done. Most teachers I know stay at school to get things done so when they come home, they don't have work hanging over their heads."

"I will take that advice," Christa told her. "I knew we

had to meet with Jubilee today, and I felt guilty about staying later."

"No guilt allowed." Glenn was tucking tiny puzzle pieces into a thousand-piece puzzle on an old oak table. "That's the plus side of being here. The kids are in good hands. The rest works out."

"And about that." Christa sat up and leaned forward. "I know you two are generous to a fault, but I need to pay you for childcare. Or rent. Something. I can't just sponge off your hospitality. That goes against everything I've worked for."

Darla sat forward, too. "Except you didn't come to Golden Grove expecting to become an instant mother of two."

"True, but—"

"And even if you've been estranged from your aunt all this time, it's hard to face the loss of a loved one," Darla pressed on. "What you're facing was totally unexpected. You didn't imagine that your aunt would be gone, or that she'd left orphaned children. Facing that loss isn't easy, Christa, even with the span of years that separated you two. It's good to give yourself a little time to adjust. Fortunately, Glenn and I are retired, so maybe it's worked out for the best. Give yourself time to grieve the childhood friend who shared everything with you while you get to know the boys."

"It's hard for me to process all that," Christa admitted. "The kind and sharing child Marta was versus the mother who chose drugs over two precious babies."

"That's when we trust God to sort the details." Darla's advice was given with grave sincerity. "Whatever demons Marta faced, they must have been fierce to have

her do such an about-face. We don't know the circumstances. We don't judge. We simply grab hold of what's
good and right—"

"Those two boys."

"Yes. And we do our very best for them. I expect
you probably have plenty of expenses on your plate
right now."

Christa couldn't deny it. "I figured the first year
would be tight while I reestablished myself in a new
area."

"If you can humble yourself to accept our help, that
would be the best gift you can give us in return," Darla
assured her. "Glenn and I were just talking about how
odd it seems not to have little ones in the house now
that Nathan is off to school, so having you and the boys
here is perfect."

Christa wasn't sure how perfect it was, but the genuine-
ness of their offer rang true. "Thank you. I've never had
money per se, and this is my first full-time teaching job
in a public school, so the salary that seemed marvelous
for a single woman in a studio apartment isn't quite the
same for my new role and a bigger place. You guys have
blessed me, and if there's anything I can do to help you,
I will gladly do it."

"You're doing that just by being here. And letting us
help with the boys," Glenn told her. Then he aimed a
mock fierce look in her direction. "As long as they stay
away from my puzzle."

She laughed. "Then we better tie up the chairs, because they're both climbers. I'm going up." She stood,
stretched and yawned. "If I start my prep right now, I

should be done by ten. I'll see you guys in the morning. And thank you again."

Glenn shot her a thumbs-up from his puzzle.

Darla waved her thanks off. "Our pleasure. Go. Get some well-deserved rest."

She went upstairs. Peeked in at the boys. Jeremy was all arms and legs, his body splayed across the sheets.

Jonah was curled up on the inside, cocooned in a cozy little throw.

But the image that played with her brain wasn't a visual of sleeping boys. It was of Tug, cradling Jeremy like you would a much younger child, letting the boy feel safe and sound in *Copper Guy's* arms. Then playing with him. Tipping him upside down.

The smile on Tug's face...

Her brain understood why she couldn't be attracted to the kindhearted, funny deputy. Her heart wasn't getting it, which meant she needed to put her emotions on lockdown. His no-romance declaration should have made the whole thing easier. It would have if she hadn't seen his declaration as a challenge. A challenge she couldn't accept, of course.

But one she'd love to win. And that right there was a conundrum.

Chapter Seven

Tug Moyer never took the coward's way out, but that was precisely what he did the night before.

"Dad, are you recording our TV interview so we can see it tonight?" Vangie asked, bounding into the O'Laughlin kitchen with her normal high-gear enthusiasm early the next morning. "I wish it was on before we go to school."

"They're emailing me the link, so we'll be able to watch it whenever."

"Sweet!" She poured herself some cereal, got out a bowl for Nathan and poured his, too. "Can you get waffles this week? The blueberry kind? And the real syrup, even though it's expensive? And can we go play with the boys again tonight? I like helping with them, and Grandma says I'm a natural babysitter."

Two questions were easily answered. The third? Not so much because the more time he spent with Vangie's new teacher, the more he *wanted* to spend time with her. "Yes, yes, and probably not because I have things to do. We're going back to our house tonight as long as the furor's died down. We need to get our lives back to normal, Vangie."

She set the cereal box down and stared at him. "But normal is going to Grandma and Grandpa's after school every day." She looked from him to Nathan as her brother yawned his way into the kitchen. "Do you mean we won't be going to their house in the afternoons because you're working at school now? Because I like going over there. So does Nathan," she insisted. "It's our thing."

"You're eight, Evangeline. You're not old enough to have a thing."

"Dad..."

"Coffee." He lifted his mug. "If you press me before cup number two, you know what the answer will be."

She frowned, but took his advice for once. Pressing her point so early in the day did neither of them any good, but with a new normal looming, she made a good point.

Would he be driving them home daily?

No. There would be days when he needed to get things done at the station house or at his school office, and the campaign was in full swing, so he couldn't be lying low when it came to his parents' place, just because Christa was there.

She drew him. And not just Christa, but the boys, too. What kind of man wouldn't be taken with those two innocent little guys?

But it wasn't the boys that set his heart racing.

It was their beautiful caregiver.

Did she know how pretty she was? How that teasing smile played havoc with his emotions? Made his palms go damp?

Even now he was counting the hours until he'd see her again.

He'd used the kids' schedules as an excuse last night, but he hadn't slipped away because of them. It was him. Laughing with Christa. Sponging off the messy toddler. Wiping her cheeks, which had put him directly in mind of a follow-up kiss.

And that thought barreled him right back around to why he avoided romance completely.

Losing Hadley.

He'd brushed off her symptoms.

So did she, which she mentioned time after time to you way back then. Just so you wouldn't beat yourself up, and yet—here you are.

He knew that, but he had shrugged off the various little signs that might have nailed her diagnosis more quickly. A more protective husband would have insisted she go to the doctor. Taken her there himself. When they realized later that those indiscriminate indications were all signs of the ovarian cancer that eventually killed her, he blamed himself.

In truth, he'd hated himself.

She'd trusted him. She'd trusted medicine. And when the first doctor prescribed some gut-calming meds, they assumed it was no big deal.

Until it was a life-taking deal, and all he could see was how casually he'd treated her health. And then she was simply gone.

"How can I wait until after your coffee if you're not drinking your coffee, Dad?" Vangie's cereal was gone.

Nathan's was half-gone. And he hadn't taken a sip from his mug, not even once. He swallowed a sigh.

"You can go to Grandma's on the school bus like always. You're right. I've got work to do, and things have calmed down enough for you to go straight over there."

"Did you have to donate all the cookies?" Nathan wasn't a morning person like his sister, but the fate of the baked goods had obviously been preying on his mind. "Even my favorites?"

"Chocolate-covered peanut butter?"

Nathan's lower lip pushed out. "That is my most favorite ever. And they're all gone."

"Grandma said she'd make some today."

His face brightened. "I love hers the most."

"I know, buddy." He slugged down his coffee and pointed to his watch. "Ten minutes until we're out the door. Brush your teeth and find anything you need. I'll gather the rest of our stuff from here and bring it home this evening."

"I'll love being at my own house." For once Vangie's tone wasn't overly dramatic. "But it would be fun to live in this house during apple weekends. I saw CeeCee in school and she says it's so busy because people are coming and going all the time."

"Busy's good. But twelve hours of traffic and people pulling in and out can't be a lot of fun for kids. Not if you can't just go outside and play."

The common sense of his words changed her viewpoint. "I didn't think of that. Can you get ice cream for tonight, too? The kind with apple pie in it?"

Typical Evangeline instant-change-of-subject.

Some days he puzzled about Evangeline's mind. The

child went through life constantly engaged, as if her brain was "on" 24/7. They used to joke that she rarely slept, and when she did, her mind was still racing because she'd wake up having mentally solved whatever problems had faced her the previous day.

Nathan's easygoing nature had almost been a relief because being Evangeline's parent overworked his brain cells. "Or we have apple pie and put vanilla ice cream from the IGA on top."

"It's all about ratio, Dad."

Hadley's words, coming out of their not-quite-nine-year-old daughter. Her science-loving mind mentioned ratios on a regular basis. Funny, he hadn't thought of that in a while, but Evangeline was quite serious.

"If the pie to ice cream ratio is off, it's not as good. Too much crust spoils the whole thing, but it has to have some crust, or it's not apple-pie ice cream. It's ice cream with apple-pie filling."

"As always, life is all about the details." He grabbed his lightweight jacket from the kitchen hook. "I'm bringing the car around to this side. Meet me in one minute."

Nathan hurried off to grab his things. He rarely kept Tug waiting. Evangeline chronically kept him waiting. So different.

It was nice to arrive at school and not be bombarded with reporters.

That lasted exactly one hour, unfortunately.

He was addressing a government-in-action class when Mrs. Menendez called him over from the high school at 9:20 a.m. "We've got a film crew here. They were trying to get a private interview with Vangie about her video. Ms. Alero intervened and I've got the crew here in the office. They are quite unhappy."

Protests of freedom of the press and free speech came through as he ran to his SUV cruiser. "Be there in two."

He looped the car around to the front entrance of the elementary school, but stopped to check on Vangie first. He knocked softly on Christa's classroom door.

She spotted him through the glass. Their eyes met.

Concern deepened her gaze. Concern, and maybe something else? Which of course set his pulse racing all over again.

He lifted an eyebrow in Evangeline's direction. Christa motioned Vangie to join them. Then she crossed the room and eased open the door. She half shut the door behind her once Vangie came through. "They were going outside for gym class," she told him softly. "I was walking back here for my planning period and I heard voices. Different voices. It sounded out of place, so I went back down the access hall and there they were. Vangie couldn't get to the door to join her class because one of them was in front of it."

So the crew had effectively blocked an eight-year-old from getting help.

"I didn't know what to say, Dad," Vangie explained. "They were asking me questions about why I wanted you to go out on dates, but not like Mrs. Brewster did when she came to the house. It was like these guys were trying to be funny, only they weren't funny. I hope I didn't say anything bad."

She was worried about him. About his image. The campaign. He crouched down and drew her into his arms. "Hey, no worries, okay? I'm on pretty solid ground, but I don't like that they didn't politely ask to talk to you. They cornered you. And how did they get into the school in the first place?" That was the real question. "Miss Ivy would never have just let them through."

"I don't know." Christa looked angry. She reached out an arm and looped it around Vangie's shoulders. "I'm going to walk her out to her class while you handle things in here. Sound good?" She posed the question to Vangie.

Vangie answered in a relieved voice. "Yes. Thank you, Ms. Alero."

"You are most certainly welcome, Miss Moyer." Christa kept her voice jovial, but the look she sent over Vangie's head—an expression of dismay—conveyed a different message. As she and Vangie walked toward the soccer field beyond the gym, he strode down the main hall to confront the reporters who thought it was okay to sneak into a school and demand answers from a kid. Because it wasn't all right, and it didn't matter if it was his kid or someone else's—it would never be all right. And he was about to make sure they knew that. Firsthand.

"So, Christa, is there anything else I should know before the department runs its normal background checks?" Jubilee tipped her glasses back up on her nose once she finished tapping something into her electronic notebook two days later. "Anything you'd like to share?"

Like to share?

No.

But if Christa was going to become a caregiver for

two impressionable boys, she wanted it to be from a position of honesty. She folded her hands and nodded. "I was arrested and charged with a juvenile crime at age fifteen. I got involved with a guy who was big into a gang and that meant I had to be part of it, too. I didn't want to lose him, so I went along with it, but it put me in the middle of an extortion ring they were running on local businesses. If the businesses didn't pay for *protection*—" she made quote marks with her two hands "—they suffered whatever consequences the gang chiefs decided. And it could be a wide range of horrible things, I'm afraid."

"What city was this?"

"Sinclair, California."

"Are the records sealed?"

"Yes. But I don't know how effective that really is. And while I wasn't physically involved with the actions they took, I was there. And that was shameful enough because I did nothing to stop them from hurting an old man. If I could go back and change things, I would. But life doesn't offer that option."

Jubilee had stopped typing as Christa spoke. Darla had taken the boys and Tug's kids to the playground to give Christa some privacy with Jubilee. Jubilee sat back slightly. "I'm sorry you went through that. But real glad you came out the other side and changed your life completely, Christa. That's a rare and wonderful thing."

"Had I listened to my mother, I could have avoided a lot of things. Including that." She made a face of regret. "Another lesson I learned too late. Will that old record mess up my chance to take care of the boys?"

Jubilee shook her head. "Those records are sealed because kids are rightfully held to a different standard, so they shouldn't be a problem at all. But," she added, and a note of caution softened her voice, "while the system *should* be foolproof, loose lips can change things. The internet provides access to media coverage, so a lot can be uncovered without getting into the actual records. Not that we would have looked further. You've had no infractions since then?"

Christa shook her head quickly. "None. It was a stupid mistake made by a stupid kid who grew up too fast. I never thought about the consequences of my actions, or how it would encourage others. I disappointed my mother, my teachers and myself. That was quite enough for one lifetime."

"They say there is only one thing worse than learning from experience, and that is to not learn from experience." Jubilee tapped the notebook thoughtfully. "I'm glad you told me, but it shouldn't be a factor, and it doesn't change who you are now. And that's what the report will examine."

Christa breathed easier.

Her teenage infraction hadn't blocked her from getting teaching assignments in California or Seattle. And she'd gotten the job here with no questions asked, letting her résumé and stellar commendations speak for her. But she hated that she was hiding something.

Would it do any good to come forward with her sordid history?

No.

But it felt dishonest. As if she were misrepresenting herself.

"And I hope you're not beating yourself up over all of this." Jubilee tucked the notebook into a carrying case.

"In my line of work, I see all sorts of people, Christa. I face some grim situations, and I'll share a grain of truth with you—the folks who've overcome the rough roads of life have a hidden strength that others might never know because it's impossible to understand some paths if you've never traveled them. Frost's 'road less traveled' option rings true, and while I'm sorry you had a rough go of it as a kid, you bring more to the table as an adult. And definitely as a teacher."

The kindness of her words eased Christa. "Thank you, Jubilee."

"You are most welcome. I'll get things in motion. And have you made decisions about your aunt? A funeral?"

"I'm meeting with the pastor of Hope Community Church after school tomorrow to plan a memorial service," Christa replied. "Something warm and loving so the boys have closure, but I can't afford an expensive funeral or cemetery plot. I hope that doesn't sound harsh."

"It sounds heartfelt and sensible," Jubilee declared. "I'll be glad to help you with anything you need. I'm sure this wasn't on your list of expectations."

"No. But sometimes what's not on the list is what strengthens us."

"Wise words."

Christa walked Jubilee outside just as Tug's car pulled in. He parked the car in the turnaround and hopped out quickly, hoisting a bag. "Ice cream. They didn't have the kind Vangie wanted the other day, but it was back in stock, so I grabbed some. Who expected such warm weather this late in September? Eighty-four degrees?"

"I'll take the warmth as long as I can get it," Jubilee told him. "The older I get, the longer winter seems."

"Did you guys get things taken care of for the boys?" he asked, his gaze seeking out Christa's.

Her silly heart did a schoolgirl dance and she had to tamp it down mentally. "Yes, the paperwork is all filled out. Have you figured out how those reporters got into the school the other day? Because I can't pretend that kind of thing doesn't worry me."

He started heading to the door to put the ice cream away. "Still under investigation. But right now ice cream rules."

"As it should." Jubilee waved, climbed into her car and pulled onto the road before Tug returned.

"Where is everyone?"

"Playground."

"Let's walk over."

A stroll through town with a handsome cop at her side.

What sensible single woman would say no to that? One with a record.

But when he started for the sidewalk, she fell into step beside him because they both had kids at the town park. Walking there together was nothing more than two parents heading after their kids.

"How was Vangie today? She asked me this morning about those reporters again. I put her off because there wasn't much I could tell her, but I don't want her worrying about it."

Kids were generally a safe topic of conversation. "She didn't bring it up," Christa replied. "Her current focus is embracing her ancestors, it seems. We were discussing local community and government today, and how the plateau was settled by pioneers, and how that flourished once the railroad came through. Vangie shared the Moyer family history of fruit and orchards. She is now determined to make applesauce like the pioneers did, so your mother has promised to teach her. But I'm still concerned how those people got into the school. Who let them in?"

"They're claiming there was an open door."

Christa rolled her eyes, because the days of open doors and schools were a thing of the past.

"I did find a doorstop about ten feet down the hall. Just lying there."

"Someone wedged the door open for them? Deliberately?" She stopped walking and stared up at him. "Who would do that? Did they pay someone who works at the school to do that?"

"I don't know yet. They denied it. They claimed they didn't realize the school had a one-door access policy, that they stumbled onto the open door—"

"That just happened to be on the corridor we use for gym class."

"And they were surprised to see Evangeline right there, as if it was meant to be."

"You're not falling for that, are you?"

Grim, he shook his head. "Someone set this up deliberately. Why were they that vigilant to get an eight-year-old's story that's already been aired millions of times on the internet?"

They were about to cross the road leading to the park, when Christa spotted a sign for Tug on the corner. But this sign was alongside another one, with his opponent's name. "Tug, what if they weren't after just another cute story about a precocious kid?"

He followed the direction of her gaze and hummed softly. "Ross's campaign? He's already insinuated that I set this whole thing up for publicity."

"Nothing like words right out of the kid's mouth to use in a sound bite or simply to add fuel to the fire. At the right time."

"You're into politics?" Her idea had sparked him, but his question surprised her.

"Not politics as much as history. I like to think of it as the making of a nation. But politics and ploys played a huge part in everything from the explorers to expansion, so it all comes together. Not always for the right reasons."

"You could be right." Kid voices drew his chin up. He spotted the kids and grinned as if dirty politics were instantly downgraded to second place. "They're having a blast, aren't they?"

Darla had Jonah in a baby swing. He was kicking his feet and shouting "More! More!" with every push of the swing. Totally carefree.

Vangie was on top of a monstrous climbing apparatus that combined primary toned metal with pressure-treated lumber to form a castle-like shape, and Vangie wasn't climbing the inside of the castle. She was nimbly scaling the outside of the structure. Christa was pretty sure she was about to fall to her death, but no one else seemed the least bit concerned, so she remained silent. Nathan was pulling himself along a rope wall, fighting for his foothold, trying to avoid the fake alligators in the pseudo pool below.

And Jeremy was off on his own.

Other kids ran around, weaving between the equipment, laughing with Vangie and shouting to Nathan.

But Jeremy had curled himself up on the far side of a twisty slide, gaze out-turned. She approached him quietly and took a seat beside him. "Hey."

He didn't look up. His eyes were down, and she saw his lower lip quiver. He fought to control it, but it quivered again.

"Did you get hurt, honey? Did you fall down?"

He didn't answer. Chin down, he swiped a dusty hand to his face. The action left muddy streaks of gray across his caramel-toned cheeks.

She wrapped an arm around his shoulders and drew him in. "I've got you, sweetie. I've got you."

He tucked his head against her shoulder.

His little shoulders shook. And when he sobbed softly, she wanted to cry right along with him.

She didn't.

She held him, letting the other kids laugh and play around them, leaving them alone in a secret sea of sorrow. When he finally stopped crying, he kept his head there, right there, tucked between her heart and her shoulder. "I miss my mommy."

Four simple words she couldn't change or erase. "I know."

"I just miss her so much. When is she coming back? Soon?"

Christa had never been one to pray spontaneously. She was an end-of-the-day prayer girl, but she changed that strategy instantly because if ever a situation needed the Lord's guidance, it was this one. Right here. Right now. What does one say to a small child who's lost his mother?

"I know you miss her. She loved you so much. You and Jonah. And she must have been so proud to have two beautiful boys. Strong and wonderful boys," she added, with a squeeze to his shoulders. Then she drew a breath and waded forth with the truth. "But, darling, Mommy can't come back. Not this time. She's gone to Heaven, and Heaven's not like other places. It's beautiful and wonderful and marvelous, but people can't come back from there."

"Ever?" His whole face—his entire countenance— begged her for a different answer, but how could she lie to him?

She couldn't. "No, but that's why God put me in your life. And Darla and Glenn and Nathan's daddy. Because he knew you would need to be loved and protected every single day and we can do that for you."

"But you're not my mom." Disbelief underscored the tragedy of his simple words.

Her heart stilled.

She couldn't mend the tragic reality on his face. "No," she told him softly. Very softly. "But your mom was my best friend when I was a little girl just your age. She loved me. I loved her. And even though I can't talk with your mom or laugh with her or share things with her anymore, I get to love you and your brother. And that's the very best gift she could have ever given me."

"She gave us to you?" Confusion darkened his gaze. "Like a present?"

"Exactly like a present. The best one ever," she whispered to him.

"Jemmie!" A happy voice hailed them from across the bright-toned play area. When Jonah hurried his speech, Jeremy's name lost a syllable. He must have spotted them from his spot on the swings, and he yelled his brother's name again. "Jemmie, I go so high! To the sky!" Jonah threw his arms skyward. "I flyin', Jemmie! I flyin'!"

Jeremy swiped his dusty hand to his cheek again. He studied his little brother, then swept a quick look over the playground with an expression that went beyond his tender years. "I always wanted to come here. When I was little."

As if four years of age was so very old. "To this playground?"

He dropped his chin and scuffled his left foot. "Yeah."

"So you lived nearby?"

He frowned as he considered that. Then he glanced around. "We would drive by and I would ask Bud to stop. He always said no. And then we didn't drive by here anymore."

Bud was a nickname for Marta's latest male friend. What a life her choices had brought to these two innocents. And what a wretched ending for her, but Christa couldn't dwell on that now. She tickled his chin with a loving hand. "Then I'm glad we can play here now."

"It's not as special as I thought. You know?" He peeked up at her.

"Things will feel special again," she promised him. "In time. I promise."

"Do we have to keep moving places? Like all the time?"

"Not once we find a place to get settled," she told

him. "We'll find a place to call home and put down roots together."

"Like a flower?"

"Yes." She smiled down at him and passed the palm of her hand across his sweet tearstained face. "Just like a flower. And we'll blossom together. You. Your brother. And me. I'm just real glad that God put me right here so when Miss Jubilee came looking for me, I was close by. Have you tried that twisty slide?" she asked in a lame attempt to change the subject.

He scanned the tall, broad red slide. "Twisty slides bump."

A blonde little girl came down the somewhat awkward slide just then, proving Jeremy right. She kind of thumped and bumped her way down, and the whole thing didn't look like that much fun.

"There's a slippery slide at another place. It's so fast. Too fast for Jonah, but not too fast for me."

"I like a fast slide myself," she told him. "Fast slides are like flying."

"And sometimes there was a puddle at the bottom and my feet splashed and that was the most fun of all."

"Jemmie!" Jonah shrieked his name again. Not for any particular reason. Just to connect with his big brother.

Jeremy stood up. He didn't hurry. He didn't smile. He looked around thoughtfully, then sighed.

His little shoulders curved inward, but then he squared them up and took a deep breath. "I'll go swing with Jonah."

"Sounds good. Do you want a swing like his?"

Jeremy eyed the bucket-style safety swing and slanted a dubious look her way. "Those are okay for babies."

He settled himself onto a standard curved rubber swing. She pushed him to get him started, and by the time the height of his swing matched Jonah's, his face had softened. He didn't grin or even smile as he soared into the air. He didn't pretend to be happy.

That was going to take a while. Christa understood the reality of grief.

But he didn't look tragic, either, and to her that was a big step forward.

Tug came their way. Evangeline skipped alongside. She peered up at her father, said something and raised a brow. Then Tug burst out laughing.

He was still grinning when they reached the swings. "Hey, guys. Anybody here want to go super-duper fast and high all at once?"

Jonah responded instantly. "I go so high! So high!" His excitement encouraged Darla's smile as she kept pushing the back of the black vinyl swing.

"Clearly his level of satisfaction has been met," noted Tug. He angled a look at Jeremy as the swing came forward. "Ever have an underdog, kid?"

Jeremy shook his head, but a quirk of his cheek showed interest. "I don't know what it is."

"It's when Dad makes you go so super high and fast that you think you're going to fall off but you don't!" declared Vangie. "They are the best pushes ever!"

"Can you hang on tight?" Tug persisted, and the boy's eyes widened in anticipation. Then he nodded.

"Real tight. I'm strong."

"Well, you need to be for one of my underdogs," Tug told him. He came around back, winked at Christa, then took hold of the swing when it came back toward them. "Ready?"

"Yes." A quiver of anticipation wiggled Jeremy's reply.

"Here we go!" Tug didn't just push the swing. He raced beneath it, across the depression in the wood chips, a hollow formed by the scraping toes of children, and when he gave Jeremy's swing one final thrust, the swing flew high and fast, fast enough that the boy rose up from the seat, just a little, and then settled back into the seat as it came backward again.

Jeremy didn't just look delighted. He looked amazed.

"Again! Again! Can you do it again?"

"I can do it all night, but we do have to eat at some point, so five more. Okay?"

"Okay!"

The sober face had disappeared. The boy's grin showed perfect little teeth. Nathan raced their way and fist-pumped the air. "I want underdogs, too! They're my favorite!" He jumped onto one of the available swings. "And my dad gives the best ones!"

In the space of moments and several underdogs, Tug had wiped the look of sorrow from Jeremy's face. It would come back. She knew that. But for this moment, the presence of a big guy who could create a really great underdog had wiped the slate clean.

The presence of a father.

She'd never known her father. She had no idea who

he was, but if she could design a picture-perfect father to help raise two little boys, he'd look like Tug Moyer.

And while that was a dangerous image to foster, it was also a beautiful one. One that wouldn't be easily erased.

Chapter Eight

Overtime tended to happen more often during apple season. The increase of traffic, the influx of people, motor vehicle accidents and having him monitoring the school on weekdays maxed out Tug's work schedule. By the following weekend, Evangeline must have realized he wasn't about to slow down and she shared her disapproval when he dropped the kids off at his mother's on Saturday morning.

"See, Dad, this is exactly what I mean." She faced him in his mother's kitchen and ticked off her fingers. "You're working all week, you've been busy every night and now you're working the weekend, too. This is why you need my help. We're never going to get anywhere if you don't take some time off. These women won't wait forever, Dad."

No deputies got time off this time of year except for family emergencies. He put a bag of extra clothes inside the small porch closet before he turned to face her. "Vangie, it's autumn in the apple capital of the world.

The sheriff's department is busy right now, honey. Give it a rest."

"I sorted out all the letters for you," she continued as Darla and Christa met them in the kitchen. She faced the women to drum up their support. "I could only read some of them, and if somebody had horrible handwriting, I just threw it away because they really should know enough to type their letters if they can't write nicely."

"You can read cursive?" Christa tucked Jonah into his high chair, set a handful of graham cracker cereal in front of him to appease him for a few minutes and aimed a look of surprise at Evangeline. "That's pretty great."

"I can only read some of it, but I couldn't even get Dad to look at the letters, so I had to do it all myself because no one would help me." She aimed a dark look up at her father.

"Vangie, there's just no time right now. Give it a few weeks. Things will calm down eventually. I promise."

"But the ladies might have found someone else by then." When she looked at him—and he noticed her chin trembled slightly—he realized this was more than a cute endeavor. For Evangeline, it was a mission, one he was thwarting.

"Vangie, I—"

"Why don't we all help tonight?" Darla asked. "Four adults and Vangie? We can get through those mail sacks in no time."

He'd have reinforcements and Vangie's efforts wouldn't go unnoticed. "Perfect. Problem solved. They asked me to work tomorrow," he began to say, but Nathan frowned instantly.

"We're supposed to pick apples at CeeCee's farm, remember?" he implored. "Her mom said we can come anytime and you said we'll go Sunday. Only how can we do that if you're always gone?"

"If you'd let me finish," Tug scolded lightly as he grabbed a handful of cookies. "I said I'm apple picking with my kids tomorrow and nothing can get in the way of that." He ruffled Nathan's hair. "So there."

"But why do you have to work all the time?" Vangie planted her hands on her hips. "Don't they have rules about stuff like that?"

"They do." He saw Christa duck her head, but not before he recognized the smile she didn't dare share. "But I took a pledge to uphold the law and being in school is an extra job right now. A job that will hopefully help what's happening with the bigger kids," he reminded her. "You know I have to work alternating weekends, Vangie. That's not new or different."

"But then you weren't working all week," she told him.

She was technically correct. He generally had a day or two off midweek when he was working the weekend rotation, but those days were often call-in days. He minimized overtime when the kids were home over the summer, but gladly accepted the extra hours once school started in the fall. "You didn't notice because you were in school," he told her. "In any case, duty calls. Be good for your grandparents and we'll go apple picking tomorrow. Maybe Renzo and the girls can join us. The later apples should be almost ripe," he added with a glance toward the calendar. "Christa, what do you think? Can we take the boys to my friend's orchard and pick some apples? Buy some fresh cider and fried cakes?"

"That sounds marvelous, so yes," she replied. "Count us in. Then Darla can show us how to make applesauce. I've never made anything like that," she added to his mother. "I'm excited to see how it's done. And with so many helpers, it should be quite the adventure."

He didn't miss the wry note on the phrase *so many helpers*, but when he looked her way, the bright smile said she was actually looking forward to it.

"It's a date," he declared. The minute the words came out of his mouth, he kinda wanted it to be a real date, so when she lifted her gaze to his, he smiled. Yeah. That kind of smile. He didn't wink, but when she tossed him a scolding face, he knew he didn't have to wink.

She got it.

He kissed his daughter goodbye, did the same with Nathan and headed for the door just as Jeremy skidded into the kitchen and aimed straight for Tug. "Hey, you!"

Tug grabbed him up and semi-tossed him into the air. When Jeremy shrieked a little, Tug grinned. "I thought you were still sleeping."

Jeremy shook his head so hard his hair danced. "Can we swing today? Like before?"

"When I get home later, okay? If that's all right with Christa?" He looked over the boy's head to catch her eye.

"If it doesn't rain," she warned Jeremy. "If it does, we have to wait because underdogs are hard to do when it's slippery."

"And it's hard to hold on to the swing," Tug reminded him. "So if the weather's good, we'll go to the park and swing, okay?"

"Okay." The boy aimed a very serious look at Tug, then leaned close. He tried to whisper, but four-year-olds weren't the best whisperers on the planet. "She tried to do underdogs." He slanted a look at Christa, who was pretending not to overhear. "Only I went all crooked and almost hit the bar, and then we changed to a middle swing and I still went all crooked, but I didn't hit the bar. Just another swing. So that's why we need you."

Tug choked back a laugh. "I'll make sure it happens, my friend. I promise. Apples and underdogs." He set Jeremy down and jogged to his car.

Was he taking on too much again? Or was this simply an unfortunate combination of circumstances?

The sheriff's campaign was well on its way. Vangie's internet ploy had created a situation that needed attention, but that seemed to be dying down. On the other hand, he understood what most others didn't. He hadn't ended up as the school resource officer because of a breach of protocol. Sheriff Wainwright had slipped him into place as part of a plan. Citing his actions with the boys gave them an excuse to put him into place without putting their on-site middle-school investigation into the spotlight. Yes, he'd broken through a door to save those boys, he and Renzo both. Yet he couldn't renege on the resource-officer job because he'd gotten a glimpse at what was going wrong inside the middle school, and if the board removed him now, all his inroads would be lost.

Vangie was right. He was gone too often and too

long, and he'd promised himself he'd never do that again when Hadley got sick.

Yet here he was. Playing superhero as if no one else could get things done.

An incoming call put an end to his speculation. He took the call on his dashboard connection. "Moyer here."

"It's Renzo. Are you clear?"

That was code for wanting to make sure no one could overhear their conversation. "Yes."

"Those reporters that got into school through the propped door? The ones who questioned Vangie in the hall?"

"Yeah?" He'd deliberately taken himself off that investigation because when it came to the safety of his kids, he couldn't stay neutral.

"A major donor to Ross Converse's campaign was behind it."

A knot began to form at the base of Tug's neck. "What do you mean *behind it*?"

"They had someone wedge the door open to let the crew have access, told them what time Ms. Alero's class came down that hall. That way they'd have a chance to talk to Vangie."

"But why?"

"You haven't read the morning paper?"

There hadn't been time to even think of reading a newspaper or scanning headlines on his phone. "No."

"I put one on your desk. Basically Converse is accusing you of using your daughter's cute video as a campaign ploy to curry favor with the voters."

"Converse is a moron."

"Agreed. But right now he's got the press's ear because his father and the senior editor's father were college buddies and still golf together once or twice a week when the weather's decent. That means he's got an in. An in you don't have with the local paper."

"Why should I need an in if I've got a great record and can do the job? That should be enough, shouldn't it?"

"It should be, but if he can slant the newspaper to make it look like you're using your kids to buy votes, that makes you look bad."

"Or really, really smart," joked Tug. "I'm actually a little sad that I didn't think of it."

"This might be more serious than you think, Tug."

Lorenzo had been his partner for over eight years and his best friend for three decades. They'd run the gamut together, ever since their parents became friends as they provided foster care to children in peril, and there was no one on the force that Tug respected more than this man. "I hear you, Renzo. I get it. But if I can't win the job on merit, then maybe it wasn't meant to be. You know I don't play games. If Converse wants to fire arrows at each other's families, I won't engage in the battle. If he wins votes by doing that, then I'm not the man for the job. If I don't play fair, I don't play at all."

"I hear you. And I support you. But when the reporters question you, make sure you have an answer ready. In the meantime, I'm going to make sure the donor that arranged to have that school door blocked open is going to regret passing money to a teacher's aide who is having a very rough time meeting her financial obligations since her husband was diagnosed with cancer. They picked a vulnerable person on purpose. And if that's the kind of finance guy helping run Converse's campaign, you can be sure there are other sharks in the water."

Too many sharks, from the sounds of it. Why did Converse need all that background support to win a county sheriff's job?

The pay grade was commensurate with the added responsibilities, but Converse had retired from his previous job with a hefty pension. Did he just want back in the job? Or was there more to it?

Converse had been a police chief outside of Seattle until three years ago when he moved to an upscale development overlooking the river in Quincy. You didn't live there unless you had money, and if you had money, what was the appeal of the sheriff's job? Maybe early retirement didn't suit him? Or was there another reason? "That's some mighty big guns to bring to a backyard scuffle."

"Agreed. I'm going to quietly examine why he's pulling out all the stops," Renzo replied. "Maybe that's the way they do things where he used to work, but it's not how stuff gets done here."

Tug turned into the station-house parking area. "Don't get yourself into trouble. If he ends up winning, you don't want your boss to be your enemy."

"And I don't want a crooked guy who plays kids to be my boss," his partner told him, and he didn't hide the cheerful note in his voice. "We're more wholesome here. That's how it's been. That's how it's going to stay. You wanna do a fall barbecue tomorrow?"

That sounded great. "Yes. But first we're going apple picking. Why don't you come along? Bring the girls."

"Naomi's not feeling good, so I'll take a pass on that," Renzo replied. Naomi was one of the triplets. "The girls love to share germs, so Mom wants them to lie low this weekend. I'll fire up the smoker at your parents' while you guys pick. That way the food can be ready when you get back."

"Sounds good," said Tug as Renzo pulled in and parked alongside him. "We can talk more tomorrow." He disconnected the call and climbed out of the car.

Renzo was right to call him covertly instead of talking at the station house. If Converse's campaign was bribing people, they might also be eavesdropping on private conversations. Both were major red flags, but Tug wasn't some fresh-faced youngster vying for his first job. He'd seen his share of political fallout over the years, but nothing like that in the sheriff's department. He'd been on the force for nearly two decades and had done well. He met Renzo in the parking lot. "Don't overstep."

Renzo fell into step beside him. "I won't have to. Converse thinks he's dealing with country hicks. He's pretty sure nothing will stick, and that's what's got me worried because what else has this guy got up his sleeve?"

Tug didn't know. With a wide economic divide between the haves and the have-nots, he wasn't oblivious to the county's problems, but if all of the departments worked together, they could continue the improvements that had already begun. And that was what made the fight worth the struggle.

"Lonely in Golden Grove?" Christa wasn't sure how she ended up sorting letters with Tug, Glenn and Van-

One Minute" Survey

You get up to **FOUR books** <u>and</u> Mystery Gifts...

Dear Reader,

Your opinions are important to us. So if you'll participate in our fa
and free "One Minute" Survey, **YOU** can pick up to four wonderfu
books that **WE** pay for!

As a leading publisher of women's fiction, we'd love to hear from
you. That's why we promise to reward you for completing our
survey.

IMPORTANT: Please complete the survey and return it. We'll send
your Free Books and Free Mystery Gifts right away. **And we pay
for shipping and handling too!** *We pay for*
EVERYTHING!

Try **Love Inspired® Romance Larger-Print** books and fall in love
with inspirational romances that take you on an uplifting journey c
faith, forgiveness and hope.

Try **Love Inspired® Suspense Larger-Print** books where
courage and optimism unite in stories of faith and love in the face
of danger.

Or TRY BOTH!

Thank you again for participating in our "One Minute"
Survey. It really takes just a minute (or less) to complete the
survey… and your free books and gifts will be well worth it!

Sincerely,

Pam Powers

Pam Powers
for Reader Service

"One Minute" Survey

GET YOUR FREE BOOKS AND FREE GIFTS!

✓ Complete this Survey   ✓ Return this survey

▶ DETACH AND MAIL CARD TODAY!

1   Do you try to find time to read every day?
☐ YES   ☐ NO

2   Do you prefer books which reflect Christian values?
☐ YES   ☐ NO

3   Do you enjoy having books delivered to your home?
☐ YES   ☐ NO

4   Do you find a Larger Print size easier on your eyes?
☐ YES   ☐ NO

YES! I have completed the above "One Minute" Survey. Please send me my Free Books and Free Mystery Gifts (worth over $20 retail). I understand that I am under no obligation to buy anything, as explained on the back of this card.

☐ I prefer Love Inspired Romance Larger Print 122/322 IDL GNP4

☐ I prefer Love Inspired Suspense Larger Print 107/307 IDL GNP4

☐ I prefer BOTH 122/322 & 107/307 IDL GNQG

FIRST NAME   LAST NAME

ADDRESS

APT.#   CITY

STATE/PROV.   ZIP/POSTAL CODE

Offer limited to one per household and not applicable to series that subscriber is currently receiving.
Your Privacy—The Reader Service is committed to protecting your privacy. Our Privacy Policy is available online at www.ReaderService.com or upon request from the Reader Service. We make a portion of our mailing list available to reputable third parties that offer products we believe may interest you. If you prefer that we not exchange your name with third parties, or if you wish to clarify or modify your communication preferences, please visit us at www.ReaderService.com/consumerschoice or write to us at Reader Service Preference Service, P.O. Box 9062, Buffalo, NY 14240-9062. Include your complete name and address.   LI/SLI-220-OMLR20

® 2019 HARLEQUIN ENTERPRISES ULC
™ and ® are trademarks owned by Harlequin Enterprises ULC. Printed in the U.S.A.

▲ If offer card is missing write to: Reader Service, P.O. Box 1341, Buffalo, NY 14240-8531 or visit www.ReaderService.com ▲

BUSINESS REPLY MAIL

FIRST-CLASS MAIL   PERMIT NO. 717   BUFFALO, NY

POSTAGE WILL BE PAID BY ADDRESSEE

READER SERVICE
PO BOX 1341
BUFFALO NY 14240-8571

NO POSTAGE
NECESSARY
IF MAILED
IN THE
UNITED STATES

gie, but here she was. "Can we arbitrarily dismiss letters that don't use your actual name?" she teased from her spot on the carpet. "Because I'd be okay with that."

"Grandma put all the far-away letters on the recliner. These are all people in Washington, Idaho and Oregon," Vangie explained as the letter sorters found places to sit on the floor. "She thought it would be easier out here in the living room. More space for sorting," she finished.

"Note that Grandma then pleaded taking care of the children as an excuse to not do this," noted Tug. He lifted a brow toward Vangie. "Fiendishly clever of her."

"Actually, Dad—"

Christa hid the smile that threatened every time Evangeline took her father down a peg.

"—Grandma said that three boys and a pile of mail is probably the worst mix ever, so she's going to read to them upstairs."

"So, back to Lonely in Golden Grove?" Christa held the letter aloft.

"I think she should at least know my dad's name if she's going to marry him," decided Vangie.

"It would be the sensible thing to do," Tug agreed. "I vote we discard all cutesy names."

"What about swimsuit pictures?" queried Christa.

Vangie frowned. "Don't they know where we live? There's not much swimming time here."

Tug choked back a laugh, but not before catching Christa's eye. He craned his neck as if straining to see the picture, right before she dropped it into the garbage can.

Then he grinned.

So did she.

Vangie thought the women in swimsuits were confused.

They weren't, but an eight-year-old didn't have to know that. Two-hundred-and-four letters later, they were done.

Some were saucy. Some were ridiculous. And some were simply kind letters of condolence. But every now and then, there was a really nice note.

"I can't believe we threw so many away." Vangie gave the meager pile of remaining letters a look of disappointment. "Should we go through them again?"

"Nope." Tug tossed another one into the trash and indicated the short stack with a jut of his chin. "We've narrowed things down to seven. I'd say we've done our job well. In matters like this, it's always good to trust our instincts."

"I don't get it." Vangie frowned, then yawned, then frowned again.

"If something doesn't attract you from the beginning, it's not going to work out," he explained.

She rolled her eyes, typical eight-year-old. "You can't possibly know that, Dad. Can he, Christa?"

The last thing she wanted was to be put on the spot concerning Tug Moyer's love life. "Leave me out of this. I'm just clerical help. Advice for the lovelorn is above my pay grade."

"Huh?" Vangie looked confused, but Tug laughed out loud.

And then he looked across at her. Caught her attention. Held it. Smiled. Then said, "There should always be a spark, Vangie."

But he wasn't looking at his daughter as he said it. He was looking at her.

Just her.

"An attraction," he went on. "If it doesn't exist, there's no reason to spend time going out. Doing things together. Because the attraction needs to be there."

It was there, all right.

In the beating of her heart. The skip in her pulse.

His smile grew.

She should ignore it. Avert her gaze. Shift her attention.

For the life of her, she couldn't. Or wouldn't. Because looking at Tug, meeting his gaze, letting his eyes smile into hers didn't just feel right. It felt perfect, even if she knew it was about the most imperfect thing in the world right now.

And still she gazed back and smiled because smiling at Tug seemed way too right to be wrong. No matter what she'd done fourteen years ago.

Chapter Nine

Christa studied the sloping apple orchard, the four kids, then Tug late Sunday morning. "How do you pick apples and keep the kids close by, because one minute of distraction means Jonah or Jeremy have disappeared into the wilderness at the back of the orchard."

His laugh reassured her. "It's a creek bed, but the creek's just a trickle right now. In answer to your question, we divide and conquer."

"The words of a true general."

"I do like taking charge," he admitted. "How's this?" he asked. "Vangie and I will take Jeremy. You and Nathan keep an eye on Jonah. If he plunks himself down to eat an apple, all the better." He polished a Gala apple against his soft-knit pullover and handed it the boy.

"Can he chew the skin?" she asked because she'd always peeled the skin off apples at Tug's parents' house.

"We'll soon find out."

He threw her a rogue grin, but must have taken pity on her when she cast a worried look because he nudged her shoulder. "He's almost three. He's got molars, right? He's going to do fine."

To prove him right, Jonah wasted no time taking a tiny bite of the apple. Then he peeked up at her and Tug and flashed a mouthful of baby teeth.

Oh, that smile!

Being younger, Jonah didn't seem as affected by the loss of his mother. Or maybe it was his more easygoing personality. He was like a friendly puppy, loving on everyone. It wasn't that he didn't miss Marta, but he wasn't consumed by it.

Jeremy was a different story. He went along with Vangie and Tug when they moved to the Granny Smith row to fill two baskets specifically for applesauce, but as she watched, he kept glancing around. Looking for something. Or someone. He was a lost soul, and while he tried to have fun, the effort was a struggle.

That lasted until a fluffy black-and-white dog trotted into the area, followed by an eccentrically dressed little girl. "Hey, Nathan! Me and Dreamer wanted to come see you guys! I'm glad you came to our farm again!"

"CeeCee!" Arms out, Nathan raced down the row. "My dad came, and our friends came, too, and some other friends were going to come but they got sniffles, so they couldn't, and we're gonna make applesauce with Grandma and I love your dog so much because he's the best dog ever, right?"

Nathan wasn't the only one enamored with the shaggy dog. Jonah looked surprised and a little discomfited to see the big dog.

Not Jeremy.

His eyes went wide, and the moment Nathan dashed

for the dog, so did he. "That's a big dog." He moved close, but not too close, and he looked back at Christa. "He might be a really big dog, maybe bigger than Mr. Finn's dog. Only that one was just a black dog. This dog is black and white all over. Can I pet him?"

Mr. Finn's dog. A clue to where the boys had been living? Definitely something to run by Tug later because nothing had been uncovered so far.

A tall square-shouldered man followed CeeCee at an easy pace. He caught Christa's eye and nodded assurance. "Yup. Go ahead." She set her basket down and moved toward the dog.

"I don't have experience with dogs. That probably sounds funny to you guys." She reached out to touch Dreamer's fluffy fur and the dog panted happily. "He's so soft."

"That's because he had a much-needed bath yesterday after a near go-round with a skunk. He missed a direct attack, but it seemed prudent to bathe him. Just to be sure. I'm Jax McClaren." He extended a hand. "Nice to have you here."

"Christa Alero." She shook his hand and smiled. "I'm the new third-grade teacher at Golden Grove Elementary. I've taught kids about dog safety, but you didn't generally see dogs like this where I was raised. And the dogs you did see were best avoided. I've kind of shied away from dogs ever since."

"We tend to like country dogs here," said Tug. He'd brought his hand down to pet the big dog and set it right next to hers when she stroked the dog's smooth fur again. It was a working man's hand, strong and broad without a hint of polish, a hand that rescued little boys from danger and dealt with the seamier side of life, all in a day's work. "Dreamer's a great name. That you, CeeCee?"

The girl nodded happily. "I always wanted a dog named Dreamer, and I told Mr. Jax and I told Mom and I told Grandpa, but we couldn't get him for a long time. And then we all got married and Dreamer came to the wedding. And he was mostly good."

Jax winced slightly. "I did have to replace two pew bows for the florist, but he did okay for a young dog."

"Well, I think he's so beautiful." Nathan was rubbing the dog's head and the dog was loving the attention.

"Nathan, do you want to come help my dad and me get more apples? We have to take them to my mom at the other barn."

"I can help?" His eyes shot to Tug's instantly. "Can I, Dad? I love being a farmer!"

A hint of sorrow darkened Tug's expression, but he nodded. "Of course. He won't be in the way, Jax?"

"No more than the kid and dog already tagging along." Jax winked at CeeCee and she laughed. "The more the merrier."

CeeCee caught Nathan's hand and they dashed toward the new barn. Dreamer raced alongside them, an image Christa would never forget. Kids. A dog. A full, ripening orchard. A barn.

How she wished her mother had lived long enough to enjoy this side of American life. The pastoral grace of country living. And yet Margaretta Alero made her choices purposely, to give her unborn daughter the best opportunities she could. Her sacrifice came with blessings, and Christa would never forget that.

"Where did you grow up, Christa?" Tug asked the question easily, but she didn't miss the hinted curiosity.

A part of her wanted to skirt the truth because the truth would put him closer to her history, but when she looked into his eyes, she couldn't do it. "Central California. Sinclair," she added. "My mother came here from Guatemala when she was pregnant with me. And she brought her baby sister along. She was going to raise us with all the opportunities that America offers, but my aunt had a mind of her own."

His jaw firmed. "Temptation surrounds kids these days. We face that even here in our small town. We have some isolated troubles here and there…"

Vangie and Jeremy had gone back to picking apples, and when Vangie found an especially big one, the surprise on Jeremy's face made her smile. But Christa didn't want to get into discussions about gangs and violence and such. That hit too close to home.

But that didn't stop Tug from continuing. "And that's been one of my jobs on the gang task force, to break things up before they take too strong a hold."

Like a light-bulb moment, his job in the school system suddenly took on a different note. "So they didn't put you on school duty just because of Vangie?" She kept her voice soft so the kids wouldn't overhear.

He rubbed a hand down his neck and sent her a rueful look. "As cute as she is, the county doesn't pay me to be a personal bodyguard to my own kids. Saving the boys gave the sheriff the perfect cover story to tuck me where I was needed without making it look obvious. Our proficiency rates in the middle school have dropped for two years in a row. We know that there's gang activity in the middle school and my job is to figure it out and come up with a solution."

"A one-man band?" That sounded pretty impossible.

"No. But one man to assess from within."

He dropped his gaze to Jonah. "I'm glad you're here. For the town. For *them*. I know this was unexpected. Yet you still accepted the challenge."

"Were there other options?" Brows raised, she intimated there weren't.

"There are always options. Which makes it nice when someone says yes so quickly."

"I've seen a lot of broken families over the years." Her life had been surrounded by single moms and absentee dads. Grandparents raising grandkids, trying to do their best. "If I can give these boys the life they deserve, that's a blessing. But I am constantly amazed at the amount of things I don't know about raising children." She lightened the conversation by pointing at Jonah. The little guy's face was a mess of apple juice and good old country soil. "Like remembering to bring wipes for sticky faces and hands that are now coated with dirt."

"The sticking factor of dirt to apple juice has science-lesson potential." He laughed at the little boy, then motioned toward the barn. "I'm sure they've got paper towels or something in the barn."

She might not have thought of wipes, but she'd brought tissues. "Hold that thought." She crossed through a creek bank that was both narrow and thick with growth, dampened the tissues with creek water and came back.

"Nature comes through. And creative parenting."

Approval laced his tone, and when she tucked the used tissues into a side pocket of her small bag, she met his gaze.

He smiled.

She smiled back.

And then his eyes softened, as if he liked gazing at her. Being with her. And she was pretty sure her expression said the same thing, as if that look meant more than a simple connection because for the life of her she couldn't drag her eyes from his. Worse…she didn't want to.

She did it anyway, because she had to. "Did we decide on just one basket of these Galas?" She shifted her attention to the trees deliberately.

She didn't glance over to see his reaction. It didn't matter. If he cared, she couldn't pursue it. If he didn't, she didn't need the ego bust. She palmed the fruit carefully and picked perfect lunch-box-sized rose-toned apples.

"Let's do two. They're good keepers."

He rejoined the kids and went back to picking apples as if they hadn't just shared a moment. Maybe they hadn't. Perhaps the attraction was all on her side. Whether it was or wasn't, it couldn't go anywhere, so that made it a nonissue, except when she was near him. Spoke to him. Laughed with him…

Then it became an issue, after all.

They finished picking a few minutes later. Vangie ducked through the trees. "Dad said I should help you carry these because it might be tricky with Jonah."

"Your dad is right." She took Jonah's hand in hers

and hoisted one basket of apples while Vangie carried the other one. "That's not too heavy for you?"

Vangie brushed her question off in a move just like her father's, willing to go the distance. "No way. It feels good to be picking apples again. We used to do this when me and Nathan were little."

"Nathan and I," called out Tug from his row, parallel to theirs.

"Grandpa owned the orchard right next door to this one, but then he wanted to retire and he sold it to Mr. McClaren's family. I was little, so I probably wasn't a lot of help."

The sound of a snort-laugh came through from Tug's side of the fruit-laden trees.

"But I *tried* to help," Vangie went on, "because Grandpa was busy all the time."

"Apple season is three months of nonstop work," Tug added as they met at the gravel drive separating the orchard from the barn. "And normal work the other nine months of the year."

"You can say that again," noted Jax as he drew close again. He and the kids had finished loading bins of apples onto the bed of his white pickup truck. "September and October run us ragged around here between school field trips, apple tours and apple picking, but we wouldn't have it any other way. Our family's major fruit enterprise is very commercial. Keeping O'Laughlin Farms hands-on gives us a way to keep kids connected with nature."

"And when my baby sister gets born, she can help us," CeeCee exclaimed. Then she shared an adorable concern that had Christa fighting back a laugh. "Only she might be a brother, but I told God I wanted a sister because I never had one before."

"You've never had a brother, either." Jax aimed a quizzical look down.

"But Dreamer is a boy, and he's like a brother, so we really need a girl in the family," CeeCee explained. It was clear that her explanation made perfect sense to her.

"My mom said I wanted a sister, but I got a brother." Vangie set her basket down and poked Nathan. "I got used to him. After a while."

Nathan made a face, then pointed to the little boys. "Now we've got little buddies that are living at Grandma's house, so it's like we've got a lot of kids."

"'Cept I'm big. He's little." Jeremy folded his arms in a stance much like Tug's and braced his legs. "I'm this many." He held up four fingers. "But almost this many." He switched his hand to show five full fingers.

"Have you got a birthday coming up?" asked Jax, and Jeremy nodded.

"I think I do because there were always red apples on my birthday."

Christa exchanged a questioning look with Tug. The boys' records indicated Jeremy turned four in August and Jonah would be three in February. It seemed odd for Jeremy to be confused about a birthday, but he was young. Maybe that was normal, but there weren't any red apples around the Pacific Northwest in early August. Not in abundance, anyway.

"CeeCee wants to know if Nathan can stay awhile longer. And you know we can always use an extra set of hands this time of year."

Tug slipped Jax the money for the fruit they'd picked

and nodded. "He'll love it. He loves working with the apples. He makes sure to remind me of that on a regular basis."

"Then he's come to the right place." Jax motioned to CeeCee and Nathan. "Okay, you two, go hop into the cab of the truck. Dreamer likes to ride in the back."

"Okay!" CeeCee and Nathan piled into the front of the pickup and their peals of laughter rang out through the open windows.

Jax had taken his baseball cap off to swipe his brow from the growing warmth of the day. He settled it back on his head and fist-bumped Tug. "Glad you came by today. CeeCee loves having Nathan around." Still smiling, he turned toward Christa. "And nice to meet you, ma'am. Your little boys are mighty cute."

She was about to thank him for the kind words, when Jeremy cut in.

"We're not hers." He'd recrossed his arms. He didn't loosen them, and he didn't take his eyes off Jax. And then he uttered words that broke her heart. "We're not anybody's." He turned and didn't simply walk back toward Tug's SUV. He trudged, chin down, the weight of the world firmly on the back of his shoulders.

Christa didn't hesitate.

She intercepted him, squatted down and pulled the reluctant boy into a big firm hug. "You *are* mine. Absolutely mine. We'll get all the legal stuff taken care of and that might take a little time, but make no mistake about it." She leaned back and locked eyes with him. "You are my little boys now and I will love you every single day and every single night and twice on Tuesdays because everybody should get extra love on Tuesday.

Don't you think?" She posed the question as if it was of great importance and Jeremy didn't disagree.

"I don't know. Maybe?"

"Exactly. And your auntie Christa will be on hand with whatever you need. We're family, *chico. Familia.*"

His expression changed. It went softer. "My mom called me *chico* sometimes."

"Because it means *little boy* in Spanish. *Español,*" she explained to him.

"Do you know Spanish?"

"*Si, hablo Español y Inglés. Tu mamá me habló en español cuando era muy pequeña.* Like you," she added in English. "When I was little, your mother used to teach me things. She lived with me and my mother."

"Where is your mother?"

Jeremy's question expected an answer, which meant her moment of truth had come. "She went to Heaven a few years ago. I still miss her. A lot."

He stared up at her. Maybe it was her admission about her mother, or maybe it was simply mutual understanding, but he offered a grave nod. "Like me."

"Just like you."

He sighed.

Part of becoming a teacher meant studying the developmental stages of childhood. She'd aced those courses, but seeing this child's reaction to loss and grief was more effective than months of classroom theory.

He was a real child with heartfelt sorrow, and as she glimpsed the long road before them, for a moment she felt overwhelmed. She remembered the cross. How her Savior had been so cruelly treated, then forced to drag a cross through the streets. If the sweet Lord could take all that on for her, she could surely do her best for two sweet innocents, bereaved through no fault of their own.

She picked him up. It wasn't easy because he was a sturdy boy, but she scooped him up and held him like you would a younger child. "I love you, little man. And I'm so glad I was right here when you needed me."

He hugged her back this time.

Not for long, and he said nothing, but the hug was a beginning. She was about to ask him if he was ready to go home, but then stopped herself.

He didn't have a home. Neither did she. And that was something she needed to rectify soon, she realized, because if nothing else, a child should always have a place to call home.

And for two homeless waifs, that reality was probably more important than ever.

Chapter Ten

Converse's supporters were spreading innuendo about Tug, the wannabe gang members in the junior high were more firmly entrenched than Tug had originally believed, and Christa was searching for a new place to live with the boys. With her first-year teacher's salary, there weren't a whole lot of places available. Not in the countryside, at least. There were some spots in and around Quincy, but she wanted to stay in the Golden Grove area.

He wanted that, too.

Maybe that was the biggest surprise of all.

When a possible and fairly obvious solution popped into his head, he made a few phone calls and stopped into her classroom once classes were over the following Friday. She was bent over a notebook, so he tapped softly on the door. She looked up. Saw it was him. And then smiled.

He did, too. Instantly.

It seemed like he couldn't stop smiling when she was around. He knew what he'd promised himself after

Hadley died. He'd forged ahead, feeling like he'd made a complete mess of things because he should have tried harder. But as he smiled at Christa, another thought came to him.

If he truly believed that the Lord numbered the days of His people, was he second-guessing God's directives by not forgiving himself?

He'd gone through three years of not looking left or right, and not caring to, either. Now he did. He walked into the classroom, pulled up a plastic chair, turned it backward and took a seat. "I think I have a solution for your real-estate problem, if you don't mind crazy busy weekends for the next few weeks or waiting a few weeks to move into an affordable and nice three-bedroom house near here."

"There is no such thing as affordable and three bedrooms near here. Or even two bedrooms," she scolded him. "I've looked, and the gal from the real-estate office has looked, too. Anything I can afford is either in a sorry state or in troubled areas." He read her expression, a look that said she never wanted to live in a troubled area again. "If I was five years further into my career, it would be different. A higher income opens a lot of doors. And if I'd stayed in Seattle, I'd be making considerably more money, but I don't want to live in the city, anyway. Although if I have to, I can make it work. I can make anything work."

"What if I said that my offer is move-in ready right now?"

She frowned. "Don't toy with me, Tug Moyer. Does this place really exist?"

"The O'Laughlin house on the apple farm." He

watched her eyes widen as she realized what he meant. "The kids and I stayed there while the press was hounding me. It's a great old place but it does have a couple of drawbacks. It'll be swamped with people on weekends until the weather turns, and that means the kids can't just play outside because there's too much traffic in and around the orchard for the next month. But once that's done, it's calm and peaceful and clean. And safe, Christa."

"I'm not sure how a house could be rented out that affordably." Doubt furrowed her brow.

"Did I mention it's furnished?"

He hadn't thought her expression could get more surprised and hopeful. He was wrong.

"What's the catch, Tug?"

He shook his head. "No catch. Jax's family is wealthy. They're keeping the O'Laughlin orchard as a throwback experience for families and schools to visit because it was Libby's childhood home. They don't need a lot of rent money, and they only rent it out to help others. You can have it as long as you need and/or want. Including utilities."

Her mouth dropped open in disbelief. Her very pretty mouth, he realized. Of course, there wasn't a thing about this woman that he didn't find attractive. *Not just attractive*, his brain chimed in. *Gorgeous*.

He waited for her reply.

"That's impossible."

He made a face that said it wasn't.

"Tug, are you subsidizing this? Because I can't let you do that. I am determined to pay my own way," she insisted. "It's how my mother raised me, and it's the right thing to do."

"No, ma'am, although that thought did come to mind," he admitted. "It's like I said. Jax and Libby don't need the money per se, and they wouldn't just rent it out to rent it, but when folks need help, it's available."

"And quaint and lovely."

He grinned. "It's quaint, all right. I prefer bigger rooms myself. More open. But the little guys won't care about that, and the O'Laughlin family took care of it, even during hard times. Shall I tell them yes? And if so, when do you want to move in? Before apple season ends? Or after?"

She hesitated, then set her pen down. "Before. I think it will be fun to see folks coming and going, and a good lesson for Jeremy. Speaking of the boys..." She picked up the pen again and started tapping it against the desk-top. "Jubilee is about to stop by and she didn't sound happy. She warned me that it wasn't good news."

"Worse than we've had so far?" He wasn't sure how it could get worse for those boys, but he found out quickly when Jubilee came into the room a moment later.

"Tug, I'm glad you're here, too."

She looked tired and Jubilee Samson never looked tired. In all his years of knowing her, the heavyset so-cial worker was a bundle of activity and warmth. If he were the one doing the rankings, Jubilee would get the county's highest honors, because she put the kids first, even when legalities tried to thwart her. Somehow the middle-aged African American woman maneuvered her way around a convoluted system and had scores of successful adults to her credit, people whose lives she'd touched over the years.

But today she looked worn. She pulled up a chair like the one Tug had grabbed and sat down heavily. Then she quietly opened a folder and passed it to Tug and Christa.

He moved his chair closer to Christa's so they could read the papers together. He breathed in the scent of her. She smelled of chalk dust and crayons and some kind of vanilla mix. Cinnamon, maybe.

And when tears began slipping down Christa's pretty cheeks, he did what he'd been wanting to do for weeks. He reached out, drew her in and held her. Letting her cry…

And letting her know she didn't have to cry alone.

He indicated the slim folder with a glance down at the photo of a thirtysomething man with dark blond hair and blue eyes. "When did this man contact you, Jubilee? This Danny Adams fellow?"

Jubilee sighed. "He didn't. We had to do a thorough check into the boys' backgrounds and parentage, and while there was nothing listed on their birth certificates, at some point last week this man petitioned the courts to have him named as the father to Jonah."

"Not Jeremy?"

She blinked once, long and slow. "Jonah only."

"He wants to split these boys up? These brothers?" Christa's tears had stopped, but only because they'd been replaced by anger. "Who in their right mind would think that's all right?"

"Is this a done deal, Jubilee?" Tug gripped the folder, wishing he could trash it. Burn it. Destroy it. Better to destroy a rancid trail of paperwork than children's lives.

"No. First it must be established, and the courts must approve it, and then he has to prove he has a place for Jonah."

"How do I fight this?" Christa straightened up and squared her shoulders. "There must be some way to prevent this from happening. Isn't there?"

Jubilee swallowed hard. "If he establishes paternity, I don't think you can, sweetie. He has rights as a father."

"Except he's never been present in Jonah's life. How does that equate to rights, Jubilee?"

Jubilee splayed her hands. "Your aunt had problems. We know that. Did he even know she was pregnant? Did he even know he had a child? We won't know what actually happened for a little while. There's always a backlog of cases, and now is no exception. For the moment, the boys stay with you. But if the judge confirms his paternity, then we've got a different story being written."

Christa's expression embodied hopelessness. A hopelessness he couldn't abide, no matter what the law said. "We'll fight it, Jubilee."

The older woman winced. "I know this is hard to accept. Separating the boys, allowing the father to have his son, breaking up the family unit once again…"

"Not hard," Tug replied firmly. "Impossible. Those boys have had enough to deal with in their short lives. And now, with new hope on the horizon, with a woman who loves them and is willing to sacrifice for them, all of a sudden some guy appears out of the woodwork and wants to take one of the boys. He's brushing off their psychological well-being because he wasn't the biological father of the first one."

Anger didn't just creep up his spine. It raged forward

because he'd seen too much of this over the years. "This can't happen. It can't and it won't, because there's no way those boys should be split up. They're brothers. They've been brothers from the beginning and they can't be separated. Any judge worth his salt would agree."

"And probably would agree if the boys' mother were alive." She folded her hands in her lap. "But she's not. And that means the boys' parentage and familial rights become the question. Yes, you can fight it." She stood and faced them both. "But our laws rarely fall on the rights of children over parents and it's a long and costly process. He will most likely qualify for a free attorney. You would have to be willing to spend a whole lot of money to fight something you stand a good chance of losing. Think about it, please. And pray on it.

"I'm not saying any of this is right," she continued. The anxiety in her voice confirmed her empathy. "But I know the laws and the system, and in this case, the system might win. Unless there is some reason why this man should not have access to this child if paternity is confirmed."

Tug wanted to swear.

He couldn't, because as angry as he was, he needed to be strong for Christa. For those boys. Those precious boys he'd rescued from danger, and now here they were, thrust into yet another untenable situation through no fault of their own. "How soon will we know?"

"Not for weeks. Maybe even longer. Like I said, there's a long backlog of cases and it takes time to give everyone their day in court. I'm sorry, Christa. This wasn't something anyone on our staff anticipated."

Christa pretended calm but the white knuckles of her clenched fingers said it wasn't an easy image to maintain. "Have you met him yet, Jubilee?"

Jubilee shook her head. "Not yet, but soon. He doesn't need us on board to be declared the father. However, he will need to meet with me and be checked out before custody is considered."

"So he could be declared the father but not get custody?"

Jubilee hesitated. She exchanged a troubled look with Tug. "It's rare, Christa. The laws are firm in keeping families together unless there's a concrete reason why ties should be severed or custody denied."

"I see."

But Tug didn't see. He didn't see it at all. He knew the truth of it because he'd seen kids kept in dicey situations for far too long in his time on the force. And yet he wasn't blind to problems within the foster-care system, either.

Jubilee left quietly.

He turned to Christa.

She was staring down at the paper she'd been working on. She didn't write any more. She didn't pretend to be able to focus on number charts.

Then she stood. Slung her bag over her shoulder. She faced him. "Did you mean it?"

He didn't have to ask what. "That we'll fight? Yes, I did."

"I have no money to do this, Tug."

"We'll worry about that when the time comes. I'm not angry about this guy wanting to be a father to his child."

She drew a breath and waited.

"I'm a firm believer in father's rights. But how did this guy suddenly realize that he had a kid? Your aunt is gone. Did he know it before she died and did nothing? Because there's been no link in the news between the two boys rescued from that house on Old Orchard Road and your aunt's death before that. So how did this man put it together? Was there an information leak? Idle chatter? And I doubt that part very much, because he doesn't look like the kind of guy my colleagues would engage in casual conversation. With the three principal players gone, how did he glean this information?"

"Gossip knows no limits, Tug. You know that."

She was right, but something didn't sit right with Tug. Later, he'd dig deeper to figure out what it was. For right now, he'd focus on getting a plan in motion to help Christa and the boys through this latest entanglement. "First things first, we're going to find out what kind of a man we're dealing with."

"I grew up in a tough, tough setting. I'm pretty sure I know exactly the kind of man we're dealing with," she replied softly. "But the real question is, why does he want Jonah? What's in it for him? Because why else would you come forward now, if he knew it all along? Although maybe Marta's death spurred him to want to be a better person. Jonah's father."

"At the expense of Jeremy." Tug didn't pretend to be convinced. "Wouldn't a change of heart like that make a person sympathetic to both children? I'm glad I was here when Jubilee came over, but let's put this aside for a moment and go back to the house."

"The house." She'd grabbed her book sack and slung

it over her shoulder. "Is it stupid to do that now, Tug? If this is all up in the air? What if someone shows up for Jeremy, too?"

He couldn't imagine that, but he wouldn't have thought this current scenario was possible an hour ago, and here they were. "Let's plan for now. The rest will take care of itself. It always does."

It didn't.

He knew that. He was pretty sure that she did, too. Not everything worked out, but this guy better have a record shinier than a newly minted penny because if he was tarnished at all, Tug was determined to find out.

"I get my own room?" Jeremy stared around the comfortable old O'Laughlin house a few days later, then dashed up the stairs. "Like up here?"

"Either one," Christa told him while Tug brought in more boxes. "You're the oldest. You get first pick."

Tug set the boxes down in the living room. "Toys from my mother, some that the boys loved, others that came to her from neighbors."

The generosity of this small town had blessed her multiple times. Tug's arrangement for this cute old house and the affordable price kept her right where she wanted to be, in Golden Grove. "That's so nice, Tug."

He came back with boxes of clothing, marked with each boy's name. He took those upstairs while Vangie arranged toys on what had been a bookshelf in the small living room.

Darla texted her as Christa started putting away groceries in the kitchen.

Jonah woke up. I'm feeding him now. I know you've got a busy night tomorrow so just relax and do what you can tonight.

Christa texted back Thank you!

Darla was amazing. She was the kind of woman who planned ahead, then worked her plan. Tomorrow was Christa's first open house at Golden Grove Elementary and she wanted the classroom to sparkle and the students' work to do the same. Not perfect, of course.

She'd learned better than that as a long-term sub near Seattle. There was no such thing as perfect in the classroom, and most parents understood that. She was pretty sure she became a better teacher all around when she'd finally figured it out for herself.

She put the last bag of groceries in the fridge, then dashed up the stairs to check on Jeremy. He met her at the top, a wrinkle of worry deepening the line between his eyes. "I think I don't really want my own room, okay?"

That was a big change from his earlier excitement. "Okay, but why?"

"Jonah never was all alone in his *whole life*." He emphasized his little brother's timing deliberately. "He's little. He might get scared, okay?"

His urge to protect Jonah dredged up her fears. How would Jeremy handle it if his brother were taken away? His sensitive nature was already scoring off-the-charts with all that had happened. Surely this couldn't be part of God's plan. Could it?

She bent down and gave him a hug. "It is absolutely

okay," she promised him. "If you guys want to share a room, I am completely fine with that."

He exhaled in relief. "That's how brothers are," he explained as he went down the stairs to see what Vangie was doing. "They just like being together. That's all."

Her chest went tight.

Tug sent her a look of sympathy as he moved her way. "That's a gut grabber for you."

"It is." She could admit it to him and to his parents. They knew what was going on and they understood. "Hoping to keep Jonah might be selfish because if I was his mother or father, I wouldn't want someone else raising him. And yet that's my prayer, every day. It feels right and wrong, and I'm not sure how to justify that."

"If you were the parent in question, you wouldn't have ignored his existence for nearly three years," Tug offered reasonably.

"But if he didn't know about him, that's a game changer."

"It could be." Tug moved a step closer. It wasn't much, but it meant everything to her. Everything about Tug made her feel safer. Bolder. Braver. She'd been alone long enough to appreciate all three empowering emotions.

"Or there might be a reason he didn't know," Tug went on. "Renzo will let us know what he finds out. If there's information in the public record, we'll find it. In the meantime, we'll let the system grind its wheels slowly and pretend everything is all right. Because it could be."

His strength bolstered her. His faith inspired her. But she knew the score. She understood that battle lines had been drawn. And while she hated to think about a parent losing a fight for their child, instinct told her that Jonah and Jeremy were right where they should be. With her. Now if only the courts would come to the same conclusion.

Chapter Eleven

Danny Adams had spent most of his life not being
what anyone would call a choirboy, but he'd cleaned up
his act five years ago, gotten a job with a computer re-
pair tech firm and had been a model citizen ever since.

That meant the judge would hand the boy over to
him once paternity was established.

Tug knew it the minute he read the full report.

He felt it to the core of his being, and the part of him
that championed a person's right to their child should
have been celebrating this discovery.

He couldn't, of course.

He knew that Jonah would be devastated to be taken
away from his *Jemmie*. Jeremy would be crushed to
have another loved one disappear from his life. And
Christa would feel the loss keenly. She'd be right in
the middle of her own loss, her aunt and Jonah, and
Jeremy's grief. And how would they even know what
was happening with Jonah? Would the judge require
Danny to allow her visitation rights? Or at least keep
her informed?

Probably not, and that would break her heart. It was breaking his heart, and the boys weren't even related to him.

That didn't matter, though. He'd saved them from injury and who knows what else at the hands of a crazed man, and that rescue came with a mantle of protection. His protection. But it was a moot cause with the information in his hand.

"You have to tell her." Renzo came up alongside him, saw the report and sighed. "I don't envy you, man. Those kids already love her. And they love you. When I saw you all come trooping back from the apple farm, you looked happy, man, and you haven't been that happy in a long, long time."

"I'm happy enough."

Renzo snorted. "Tell it to the mirror. I know what I see. She makes you happy but you're still carrying a truckload of guilt over Hadley. If Hadley were here, she'd smack you upside the head. You know it. And I know it. And then she'd tell you to stop wasting time because there's plenty of life left to live."

Renzo was right, but one very important fact stood out. "Except she's *not* here."

Renzo ran a hand through his hair in exasperation. "If you were talking to a victim of a crime or anyone suffering a loss, you'd remind them that life is full of left turns and unexpected moments. You'd remind them that God's timing isn't ours. But you don't seem to be able to apply the same logic to yourself."

"It's not the logic." He gripped the paper report in his hand, then set it on the desk. "I see the logic. I just can't get beyond the carelessness of it all. And I hate myself for it."

"You know what your problem is, Moyer?"

Too many to list at the moment, so he didn't bother looking up because Renzo would tell him. In short order.

"You talk faith, but you don't trust faith. You talk the talk but can't walk the walk, because you can't believe that for some reason unknown to you, God might have had a different plan. A different timeline. Because you're always in charge. You're the plan maker, so to have God thwart you stings deep. You didn't lose your beautiful wife because you were careless, Tug. You lost her because God called her home. And that's something you just don't seem to be able to accept. I'm going to grab a burger. Want one?"

"No."

"All right."

Renzo moved off.

His words stung because Tug knew they were true. Renzo had hung a variation of this talk on him at other times. A gentler version, but this time he struck deep on purpose. Or maybe it was because this time involved Christa.

She was drawn to him.

He was neither stupid nor blasé. He read the glimmer in her eye, the dip of her chin, the hinted rosiness that deepened her lightly tanned cheeks.

He was falling for her. He knew it now, but he was pretty sure he'd known it from that first meeting, when she gave him that tough-teacher look. From that moment on, a part of him just wanted to make her smile. Hear her laugh. Share time with her. Share a life with her?

He couldn't deny that the thought had crossed his mind.

Now he had to deliver bad news to her.

Not his fault. He knew that. But still, he would be the bearer and he dreaded that. She'd moved into the bungalow-style house three days ago. He texted that he wanted to stop by her classroom once school was out. It might be easier to tell her here, before she picked up the boys from his mother's house.

Going straight to your mom's for boys. Having their picture taken tonight. I want to make sure we've got as much of them recorded together as we can get.

Pizza?

Chinese?

Her quick text back made him smile.

Lo mein and Sesame Chicken. Good?

Perfect.

She'd have hot dogs for the kids. Nathan loved Chinese food.

Not Vangie. She'd prefer a dog on a bun with yellow mustard. Her meal of choice, 24/7.

Jeremy sampled everything. He didn't hold back when it came to food, and maybe it was because food had been scarce with his mother or maybe he just knew a good thing when he saw it.

Jonah was a grazer.

Funny how he knew these two almost like his own. That meant the judge's decision might be even harder to bear than he'd first thought because each day with Christa and those boys made him want more days with them. On that, Renzo was correct. He was a plan maker and he hated that this new plan had been taken out of his hands.

A touch of eyeliner followed by a sweep of mascara, both perfect to set off the smoky-gray eye shadow that brought out the same tones in her eyes. And all because Tug was bringing supper over.

"When do we get our pictures?" Jeremy hung on the railing at the top of the stairs and peered at her through the bathroom door. "You look so pretty."

"Thank you, honey." She smiled at him through the mirror. "The photographer will post the pictures on her website and then we'll pick our favorites, okay?"

"You mean on the computer?"

"Exactly like that."

"My mom used to take pictures of me with her phone."

And where was that phone? Or any personal belongings? Was there nothing left of their life with Marta? Considering the circumstances, was that for the best? She had no idea. "Of course she did. Because she loved you."

"And Jonah, too. Both of us." So serious, as if he were convincing himself of that love.

Christa went to his side and crouched down. "She did love you. Both of you. But sometimes grown-ups have problems and don't make the best decisions. And when that happens, we pray for them. We help them. And we try to take care of things for them."

"Like you're taking care of us."

"Yes. Because we're family and I love you and I want to take care of you."

"Because we're good boys." Wistfulness colored his tone, as if he yearned to be called a good boy. She gathered him into a hug.

"You are not just good boys. You're the very best little boys I could ever imagine. Strong. Sweet." She kissed his cheek with a big loud smack and he giggled. The sound strengthened her because giggles weren't the norm for Jeremy. "And such a little cutie-pie!" She smooched him once more, then hoisted him up and spun him around. "Auntie Christa loves, loves, loves you!"

He giggled again and the lighthearted sound gave her hope.

That hope was doused with reality a couple of hours later when Tug shared Danny Adams's report with her.

Vangie had taken the boys out to the backyard. No one was picking apples and the earlier sunset created tapering shadows across the green grass. They ran around, playing a little kid version of tag with the sweet abandon of children as Tug broke the news. "Considering all this, I think the judge will decide in his favor, which means he'll be able to take custody of Jonah."

She didn't want to think it, much less say the words out loud, but she'd feared this from the moment Jubilee had dropped the bombshell about Danny's petition.

"If he's proven to be the father, yes."

"I wonder if there's a chance he isn't?" She turned from the innocence of the children and faced Tug. "I'm guessing that Marta's choices weren't always wholesome."

Tug shrugged. "The DNA tests will tell one way or another. And have you figured out why Jeremy is set on his birthday coming soon? Because I don't want him disappointed."

"I checked with Jubilee and she has the birth certificates in her folder and confirmed the dates. And she said little kids were known for being *almost the next year* from the time they have a new birthday, so maybe that's why he thinks he's almost five. People do half birthdays all the time for kids in school. If they have a summer birthday but want to bring in a school treat, we let them do it on the six-month date. We could do that for Jeremy so he's not disappointed."

"If it makes him feel good, I don't care how we spin it, Christa." He moved closer so he could see the kids through the back window. They darted here and there, being children. And when Nathan would tag Jonah to be "it" because he could easily avoid the little fellow, Vangie would let Jonah tag her instantly. Then she'd chase down her brother to teach him a lesson. And not one of them seemed to mind being "it."

"They're beautiful together. Have you noticed that?" He whispered the words from behind her, but dropped his head just enough that his breath tickled her ear and her cheek. It was a featherlight motion that made her long to step back, into his arms. Closer, yet not close enough.

"I've noticed." She whispered, too, for no reason because there was no one there to hear, and yet it seemed like a conversation that should be gentle and hushed. "Sometimes I think of it being that way. Staying that way."

"All four kids together?" His breath touched her ear again. Then his arms came around her from behind and he hugged her, sighing softly. "Because it's an image I can't get out of my mind. I can't deny I'd like to see how that works out, Christa. If you'd be willing to let the deputy sheriff court the pretty schoolteacher."

She turned to face him.

His gaze drew her. His scent reminded her of clear, crisp days and freshly cut wood with a hint of spice. But it was his expression that tempted her the most. Strong. Loving. Caring. With a hint of sorrow, an emotion she understood too well.

And then he leaned in. He leaned in close enough to kiss her but didn't. Was he waiting for her to meet him halfway?

He stopped waiting right then.

His lips sought hers, and when she slipped her arms up, around his neck, he drew her in closer.

Her heart raced.

So did his.

She felt the strong beat of it, heart to heart. And then she felt something else. His badge. The firm reminder that he wasn't a regular guy. He was a deputy, running for sheriff, and she knew what that badge stood for. And how in less than three weeks, the locals would elect a new county sheriff.

She knew her past could be his downfall.

He didn't.

Should she tell him now? Let him decide? And if he did the chivalrous thing and shrugged off his career for her, would he grow to resent it over time? Maybe more important, would she be able to live with herself, knowing she'd thrown him a curve?

She stepped back, withdrew her arms from his neck and shook her head. "We can't do this."

"Seems we just did and I was absolutely okay with it." He studied her seriously. "I'm a little confused that you didn't feel exactly the same way."

She did.

Oh, she did, but she couldn't tell him that. He'd already taken a bold step forward because he didn't have the whole picture. If her past was uncovered, would the district ever offer her tenure?

Probably not.

Why should they when there were so many educated teachers looking for work? "It's not that I don't feel the same way." She wasn't going to play games with him. He deserved better than that. "But I'm in the middle of so much right now, none of it expected, and I don't dare upset the apple cart any more than it already is. I've got to focus on school, on my class. I don't want to mess up this opportunity, Tug."

It wasn't an untruth… It just wasn't the whole truth.

"I need to focus on the boys. They need someone who's in for the long haul, especially with Jonah's future in question. I need time to adjust to all of this. I don't want to turn to you just because I'm in over my head with work and kids and you're a big, strong sheriff who rides to my rescue."

"I'm in favor of that image," he admitted, but a soft smile offered understanding. "We don't have to jump into anything, Christa."

Oh, she'd jump in a heartbeat if she were coming to him with a clean, clear record. She wasn't.

"We've got time. But I want you to know that my intentions are not likely to be dissuaded by time. Instead, I expect them to increase exponentially. But I understand completely." He might have understood but he kissed her one more time. "Just so you know."

He took a step back as the kids came barreling through the side door. "Are there any cookies left?"

She used Nathan's question to change the subject. "Your grandma sent a bin." She opened the plastic tub and held it out. "Two each. And then we need to get cleaned up for bed," she told the younger boys.

"But it was so much fun pwayin' outside!" Jonah's eyes couldn't have gone rounder if he tried, and when he grabbed Vangie around the middle and hugged her tight, it was the sweetest thing. "We were wike the very, very, very best team in the world!" He hugged her again, let go and fist-pumped the air with his free hand while the other hand grabbed for two cookies. "I want to play that game wif you guys all the time! And I will be the fastest catcher ever!"

"You did great." Vangie placed her hand on the little guy's head and grinned at him. "I'll be your partner anytime, little dude."

Her words hit Christa hard. She didn't dare look up at Tug, because he knew what she knew, that the boy might be taken to a new life. She swallowed hard and forced a smile at Evangeline. "You were a great partner, Vangie. We saw how you applied your speed and engineering skills to a complex situation."

Some kids wouldn't have understood her implication.

Vangie understood it instantly. "Strategy. My dad taught me that. It's all about strategy."

"A lesson well learned." Tug motioned outside. "Say goodbye, guys. We've got to get you home to bed. School tomorrow."

Then he shifted his attention back to Christa. "Thanks for having supper with us."

"Thanks for bringing it."

He grinned and started her silly heart beating in that same rapid rhythm she'd just tamped down. "My pleasure. Good night, guys."

"G'night, Copper Guy!" Jeremy hurled himself at Tug.

He never did that with her. With her, he was always a little more subdued, as if testing the waters, but with Tug, Jeremy's quick reactions knew no boundaries.

Tug hugged him. "You know, you can call me Tug," he reminded the boy. He'd mentioned that a few times before, but Jeremy shook his head firmly.

"I like Copper Guy. That's what you are, right?"

"Deputy sheriff, but close enough."

"So it's a really good name for you, I think."

Tug hugged him and winked at Christa over the boy's head. "It's a very good name for me." He bent down and included Jonah in his hug. "See you tomorrow, little man."

"Okay! I'll be ready to run again, I fink!"

Jonah dashed off for the living room as Tug set Jeremy down.

"I'll get jammies for me and for Jonah. That way we can match."

Matching pajamas. Matching shirts. Matching pants. When she'd taken them shopping, Jeremy had insisted on matching his brother. It wasn't something that she'd do all the time. Even twins weren't advised to dress alike every day, but for now, if it offered comfort to the boys to be dressed alike, she would do it. And she wouldn't think of Jonah being somewhere else, and how that would affect Jeremy. Because thinking of it was like a stab to the heart when she saw how close they were. How many separations could children take and still grow up normal?

"Bye, Christa! Bye, guys!" She'd given Vangie and Nathan permission to use her first name at home. It was silly to call her Ms. Alero when they were together so often outside of school.

"See you tomorrow."

They hurried out to the car.

Tug turned her way. He didn't try to kiss her again. Instead, he reached out his right hand and gently cradled her cheek. Her ear. Her head. "Thank you for taking a simple night and making it unforgettable, Christa."

She leaned into his hand.

She shouldn't. She knew that. But sweet desire overshadowed propriety for that moment. "I am in full agreement. And—" she reached up and covered his hand with hers "—I am grateful for your understanding."

He smiled. It started as a slow smile, and then it grew. "I'm totally understanding, darlin', but not afraid to make sure I stay in the game. Just so you know."

She couldn't help but smile back, and when he winked, her silly heart tripped over itself all over again.

How could something so right be wrong?

It couldn't. It wasn't. Except that she might hold the key to his destruction. If she could be *sure* it would never get out, then that would be different.

But what if it did?

She watched him go and closed the door firmly behind him.

Tug's reaction didn't worry her. He was loving and forgiving, and he seemed to have a greater understanding of kids' choices than most adults. It was the possible effect it would have that kept her quiet.

What if he finds out later? And you've withheld it? Love is based on trust and truth, isn't it?

She believed that wholeheartedly, but the election was short weeks away. After that, she would tell him everything and let him decide. That way she wouldn't derail his campaign.

For now, she'd stay quiet, but with Tug being present in multiple aspects of her life, that wasn't going to be easy.

Chapter Twelve

After two weeks of campaign appearances on top of work, Tug found himself wishing for election day.

He wanted it over. Yeah, he wanted to win, but the months of working and campaigning had taken their toll.

He longed for normalcy. For time to hang out with the kids and see Christa and those two precious little boys.

Jubilee had taken a sample from Jonah for the DNA testing and, somewhere, Danny Adams had done the same thing.

Tug hoped Danny wasn't a match.

Like Christa, the hope drove his guilt higher, but there was something about this man that didn't sit right with him.

Would anyone sit right at this point? his conscience nudged.

Probably not. Knowing that the guy hadn't made a move to be part of the little guy's life rubbed Tug the wrong way. He urged Jubilee to check deeply into this man's past, and he was pretty sure Renzo was doing the same thing. And on a rare autumn day off, Tug himself had gone by the regional office of the tech firm. He grabbed coffee at the shop across the street until Danny Adams walked out, got into an aging pickup truck and took off.

The guy looked like any other normal everyday person heading home at the end of the day. Nothing had clouded his record for several years. So why was Tug unnerved? Because of Christa and how this would affect her?

The big question was, did Danny really want Jonah?

He tried not to think about it, but as November drew near, each day felt like a ticking clock. If he was feeling this anxious about the results and the judge's decision, what was Christa feeling?

He was striding down a middle-school hall when Tillie Anderson came around the corner. She smiled to see him, but then cloaked the smile with a sour demeanor. Chin down, she almost went by him when he tossed the basketball in his hands her way.

"Hey." She caught the ball and whirled on him, surprised. "Wanna shoot hoops this afternoon?"

She frowned instantly. "I don't do hoops."

"Wanna keep score? I'm going to do pickup basketball teams after school and we need someone to manage the scoreboard."

A spark of interest brightened her eyes. "You mean the machine that lights up the scores on the wall?"

"Yes. What kind of time do you have before your little brother gets home?"

"An hour and ten minutes."

"So if you take the late bus home, you're okay?"

She hesitated, shuffling her feet slightly. "Will anybody come? To play, I mean."

It wasn't a big secret that the tough guys in the seventh and eighth grades were avoiding him. "We'll see." He'd announced that he was convening a schedule of pickup games. Maybe if something helped fill those empty late afternoon hours, they'd have fewer disenchanted adolescents looking for trouble.

A door opened up the hall. Two eighth-grade boys came their way. Tillie's chin dropped quickly. "I better not."

Tug wasn't one to take no for an answer. "Hey, guys, we've got open basketball after school today. My partner and I are looking for takers. He's coming by at dismissal. You in?"

The first boy scorned him with a look.

The second one darted a dark glance at Tillie, then splayed his arms. "So two big guys want to show a bunch of eighth-grade kids how tough you are by beating us at basketball?"

Tug grinned. "Feeds my ego, so yes. You ready to get hosed?"

"Man, you got the wrong boys here." The first kid scowled up at him. "I don't throw balls at no hoops."

"You could learn." Tug reached a hand toward Tillie. She passed him the ball. "The high school is starting a freshman team next year. They'll want guys ready for fall tryouts. You can learn a lot in a year."

"Then why you talkin' to *her*?" The boy nailed Tillie with a dark expression. "Tillie's going to play basketball? I don't think so."

Tug was tempted to correct his manners, but Tillie beat him to it. "First off, Royal, I can shoot hoops if I want to, but I don't want to. But I will be scorekeeper for you." She tipped her chin and met Tug's gaze. "I'll take the late bus home to get Alfie."

"See you then." Tug started away, then turned. "And, guys, you're welcome to just show up. Every day, once your teachers release you, come to the gym."

"Not gonna be much fun when nobody shows up." That was Royal talking, and when he talked, a significant percentage of the other kids listened.

Tug shrugged, dribbled twice, then palmed the ball into a one-finger spin. "One-on-one with my partner? I'm down with that. But you're welcome to join us."

The boys exchanged looks as he turned to go down the hall.

Would they show? Would anyone?

He didn't know, but if there were no alternatives to going home and hanging out with nothing to do, how could they stop the growing cycle of kids leaning toward gangs and drugs and crime?

Idle hands are the devil's workshop.

There was truth in that old proverb. Grandma Moyer had kept four children busy, and when folks would question her strained schedule, she'd point to that plaque on the wall. It was a quality his father had passed down to Tug, although he could do with a little less busy right now.

With the election so close, he couldn't wish the days by quickly enough. He wanted to win, yes. He'd worked hard. He'd be good at the job and he had the respect of the department.

But he didn't want to win at any cost, so he'd ignored Ross's jabs and stabs and went about doing his job. Right now that entailed figuring out the teen hierarchy at the middle school and quashing the negative vibes. If he could get that done this fall, he'd consider his resource-officer placement a success. And when the district superintendent agreed to a meeting about reinstating trade classes on woodworking and basic electricity, Tug hoped they'd get even more options into place because not all kids were meant for college. Would the district be able to come up with the funds? Maybe not at first, but if they could garner some space and tools, they might be able to get a few of those retired farmers and laborers to step in and help kids see the true benefits of hands-on labor.

"Danny Adams is a match, Christa." Jubilee Samson sank into the chair in Christa's classroom on Friday afternoon and sighed deeply. "I can't say what the judge will think, but I know what the law says, and if a parent has a right to a child, that right will take precedence over anything else as long as the parent is capable."

Christa clenched and unclenched her hands. The action did nothing to relieve the rising stress within. "You're sure, Jubilee?"

"Absolutely certain. Judge Bettig is horribly backlogged, so he might not get to this for weeks, but if Danny Adams pleads hardship, he might get it moved up the docket."

"Hardship?" The word made her frown. "Tug said he's got a decent job now."

"Not financial hardship. Emotional hardship from being denied time with his son. It's not uncommon and he could make a case for it, especially if Marta never revealed Jonah's existence to him."

Christa tried to keep her fingers still. Didn't happen. Stress had shown in her hand movements from the time she was a baby, according to her mother. A habit she'd brought right into adulthood. "And yet he found out. After she was gone."

Jubilee made a face as Tug came into the room. "Folks talk, same as always. Maybe there was no reason to talk about an old girlfriend before that. Death and crime can seal lips or open mouths. It all depends on the person."

Tug stuck his phone into his pocket. "I got your text, but I still don't quite believe it. First, what was this guy doing with Marta when he'd been clean for nearly two years and she wasn't?"

"We all make mistakes, Tug." Jubilee didn't seem nearly as surprised. "It's human nature. And maybe they'd had an old relationship that reignited for a brief time."

"Well, it had to be brief because Renzo has found nothing that places Danny Adams in Marta Alero's life. And that seems odd to me."

"Drug users fly under the radar all the time." Christa didn't have to pretend a calm she didn't feel. Not with these two. "I watched that happen in Sinclair. I expect it's the same most anywhere, don't you?"

"Flying under the radar is different from being un-findable," noted Tug. "I'm sure Renzo's put in a lot of effort." He settled a hip on the edge of her desk. He'd changed out of uniform to play ball with middle-school kids, and he'd come down to the elementary school dressed in warm-up pants and a black T-shirt. "What's your advice, Jubilee?" He turned her way, hands out, palms up. "The whole thing isn't sitting right with me, but I can't tell if that's because I care about Christa and the boys or if my gut's correct. Renzo got the same vibe, but there's nothing to go on. The guy's got a history, sure. But he's cleaned it up and he's been flying right for years, so that should reassure me. And yet it doesn't, so maybe my lack of neutrality is skewing my judgment."

Jubilee stood. "I'm not a fan of slick men. Never have been. And Danny's slick, all right, but he's also clean. His apartment checks out. He had a little money trouble a while back, but he cleaned that up, and as a woman who raised three kids on her own, I know that lack of funds can mess with your head. He got through that and his credit rating is better now."

"Which means he'll get Jonah." Christa stared down at her hands. "I hate that I'm so conflicted about this," she said softly. "He's the boy's father. Of course he'd want him. And I'm sure he'll take good care of him. Why else would he fight so hard to get him?" She sighed and raised her eyes to meet theirs. "I stepped into their lives to help at the perfect time, so maybe that was my role in all of this. Maybe that's why God put me here, now, so I could be a gateway. And if that was my purpose, then it was a good one. But the thought of both boys having to adjust to life without their mother and without one another has made me an emotional mess. I put on a happy face at home and in school, but I can't trust myself not to cry in between. Which—" Christa stood up then, too "—is all right, I guess. I'm saving face at the right times, and that's what we grown-ups do."

"I'll call when I hear anything about court dates." Jubilee rounded the desk and gave her a quick hug. "You just keep being you and do the best you're able with the boys. They're blessed to have you, even if it is only for a short while for Jonah. The Lord giveth..."

"And the Lord taketh away." Christa murmured the words as Jubilee left the room. Then she turned to Tug. "Right now I feel like a total jerk because I'm supposed to say blessed be the name of the Lord, but that's not how I feel. Even when I know it's right. And that makes me even more ashamed of myself, Tug."

He didn't respond with words.

Instead, he stepped in and opened his arms, and when he hugged her close, her heart didn't race like it had before.

It settled. The stress and anxiety of Jonah's fate faded in his arms, as if they could handle anything together. And when he let her go a minute later, he snagged a few tissues from her desk and thrust them into her palm. "Mop those eyes. Let's get home to the kids. I've got campaign things all weekend, but I've got two hours right now and I heard something about fried apple pie and cider at my mom's. Reason enough to hurry home, right there."

"I've never had a fried apple pie. Or a fried pie of any sort. They actually make such a thing?"

"My great-grandmother grew apples in the Ozarks and there was enough of the South in her to bring good apple stock and great recipes when they moved west.

She was a particular sort of woman." He slanted a grin down that said more. "My mother did not come into her take-charge ways by accident, and that's all I can say about that. But when Great-Grandma took a burn at how some folks were doing business in Missouri, she and Great-Grandpa sold off during the apple boom there and came west. My apple roots go deep, but the farming genes seemed to have missed me."

He swung the door open for her to let her pass through. "I always wanted to be in law enforcement, there were no other kids to take over the farm, and when my wife died after Dad's heart problems, he sold the farm and retired. Then along comes Nathan, who loves everything about apples and orchards and farming, and I'm pretty sure I pulled the linchpin right out of what could have been a solid family enterprise."

"Except maybe your parents sold the farm because they wanted to be the best support they could be to you and the kids. And your dad's health had to be a big factor, didn't it?"

"Yes. But if I'd gone into farming, maybe I'd have taken the stress off Dad. Maybe we'd have been able to keep it going strong. It's a moot point now."

"And yet you still carry the guilt like a yoke. That's got to get real heavy, Tug."

He hauled in a deep breath. Glanced down. Then he angled the exit door open for her as they approached the parking lot. "Heavy and useless. I understand that logically. It's the emotional side of the decisions that make me question."

"Except your father's one of the happiest people I've

met." She clicked her key fob, opened the back door of her car and set her teaching bag inside. "So if he's content with his choices, why aren't you? Because that might be a really important thing to think about."

Chapter Thirteen

He knew why.

It was the *what-ifs*.

The what-ifs plagued him. Not all the time, but regular enough.

"Do you second-guess yourself on the job?" she asked softly.

He shook his head. "Not usually. That would be counterproductive."

"Then why do it with everything else?" She was looking at him, and for the first time in a long time, his vision cleared.

"I feel responsible."

"For things that are out of your control."

He glanced left, then right before bringing his gaze back to hers. "Our choices affect others. There's always a ripple effect."

She leaned her back against the door she'd just closed. "I expect you've weighed your life choices carefully. That's what guardians and protectors do. They study the terrain, wanting to take care of the people around them."

"Who looked out for you, Christa?" He leaned forward and braced his arm along the top of her car, gazing down. "Who was your guardian?"

She squinted slightly. Bit back a sigh and dropped her eyes, then raised them to meet his gaze. "My mom tried. But it was hard. A new country, a new language, two little girls and endless menial jobs, always just scraping by. I will never negate her sacrifice for me and Marta. But our neighborhood was like a quagmire, dragging you down. And even the churches seemed to cringe under the weight of the hopelessness surrounding us. The whole thing was just sad."

"Exactly why I'm working at the schools this term," he told her. "So we can get rid of the quicksand and give these kids firm footing. And why I do my videos. I wish it had been different for you. And yet maybe you're who you are because of what you've seen. Dealt with. Been through."

This time when she dropped her gaze, she didn't look back. She slipped out from beneath his arm and rounded the car, then pulled open her door. "I expect we're all an accumulation of things, aren't we? Good and bad."

He wanted to delve further. See what cast that shadow of sorrow that flickered when she talked about her past, but she had enough to handle right now. "I'll see you at the house." And when she started to demur, he gave her a look that he hoped made her come to her senses. "Mom's homemade fry-pies are totally worth the trip. If you throw hot apple cider into the mix, it's nothing to shrug off."

She smiled. Then climbed into her car.

It was a fleeting smile, though. He hated that there

was nothing he could do about that—because whenever he was around Christa, he wanted to make her world a better place. But that was next to impossible with Jonah's fate hanging over their heads.

The simple goodness of his mother's pies helped.

By the time he walked into Darla's kitchen, the scents of mulled cider and glazed pie had worked their charm on Christa and all four kids.

"Grandma, these are the best ones you've ever made." Vangie licked glaze from her fingers and gave an over-the-top sigh. "I love apple-pie-for-supper night. Even better than strawberry-shortcake-for-supper night because these pies are the best."

"You have an apple-pie-for-supper night?" Christa asked as Jonah drank cooler cider from a sippy cup.

"Tonight," Darla answered. "And in May or early June, we always have a strawberry-shortcake-for-supper night. We feast on all the strawberries, sponge cake and whipped cream we want."

"That's like the best idea ever." Christa's expression was priceless. "You are creating amazing traditions."

"And memories," noted Tug as he slung his hoodie on a hook inside the door. "A lot of stuff from growing up kind of melds together, but I remember a lot of those supper nights. Like when Uncle Jack and Aunt Carol announced they were having a baby. And when Mrs. Riley finally started talking to Mrs. Boone after sixteen years of scornful looks and silence. I have discovered the amazing effects of limitless desserts on people."

"I'm pretty sure the mellowing of age helped those two ladies," Darla replied as she drizzled a thin vanilla glaze over more folded pies. "Time does help heal wounds, but a good dessert has its own healing powers, and I can testify to that."

"I've never had anything better." Christa marveled at the pie on her plate. "It's perfect. The texture, the flakiness, the fruit. This must have taken you all day, Darla. Thank you." The smile she gave his mother held back nothing. "Thank you for this, but also for setting the example of how to be a great mother. And please say you're willing to coach me along the way."

"Gladly. Here." She slipped another one onto Christa's plate. "The little guy's eating at least half of yours, and I don't do the fried pies often. But it seemed like a good weekend to think about simple, wholesome things."

"So we're not thinking of Dad's heart tonight," Tug teased, and his parents laughed.

"The docs told me that my new construction had a good twenty years of mileage," Glenn assured him. "As long as I stay on my diet most of the time, I'm good to go. If nothing else, my heart attack taught me that you can't stop living—but you should also live smart."

"And you're like the smartest person I know," crowed Nathan from a spot at the end of the table. "You know so much about frogs and toads and apples and things to do on a farm, Grandpa. I want to know all the stuff you know when I grow up, okay? Like everything." Nathan threw his hands wide to underscore his intent.

He was so different from his world-changing sister. Nathan liked peace and quiet, but when it came to farms and apples and fruit, his eyes shone. Excitement triggered his smile and enthusiasm.

"And I'm happy to share everything I know." Glenn winked at the boy. "Nothing an older fellow likes more than to have someone who wants to hear what he has to say."

His mother hugged Nathan's shoulders once she set more pies onto the table. It warmed his heart. Too soon he had to be out the door for a town meeting on the north side of the county. His kids were staying with his parents for the night, and Christa had buckled two tired boys into their car seats to take them home. He walked her to her car door and swung it open. When she'd tucked herself in, he shut the door and she rolled down the window. "This was fun, Tug. It was a perfectly wonderful old-fashioned celebration. I'm so glad you guys shared it with us. It's definitely one for the memory books."

She smiled up at him, and he couldn't help himself, even with the boys in the back seat.

He leaned down and kissed her. He knew he couldn't linger. But the kiss was long enough to remind her of his feelings. And his intentions.

Her emotions were ragged right now. He didn't want to take advantage of that, but seeing his parents laughing together and hearing his father talk about his repaired heart drove home Lorenzo's point that God numbers days. Not people.

That was a lesson he needed to embrace. "See you tomorrow." He whispered the words against her lips. She smiled.

"Except you've got the apple festival and then the Patriot's Day dinner, so you won't see me tomorrow."

"Oh, Ms. Alero." This time it was him smiling against her face. "Where there's a will, there's a way. And I promise you…" He kissed her one last time before he reluctantly pulled away. "Where you're concerned, there is a will."

He smiled.

She smiled back.

And Tug Moyer was pretty sure he was the most fortunate man in the world. Again.

Tug's campaign folks had rigged out his booth at the apple festival in the red, white and blue he'd used to define his campaign. He'd gone into this race as the favorite. He was a known entity in Central Washington. A law-and-order guy. He'd built his life and his reputation on that.

Ross Converse was an unknown in Grant County, and his former police force had been the target of several investigations over the years, two of which ended in indictments. The indictments weren't laid at Converse's feet, but the folks in rural Washington expected the guy in charge to be in charge, and believed in a "buck stops here" kind of mentality.

Tug had another leg up.

This was his town. His county. He belonged here. He'd never wanted anything else, and now God had sent a wonderful woman to him. He hadn't been looking, and despite Evangeline's efforts, he hadn't intended on looking. In the end, Tug Moyer was falling in love.

"So here's our schedule." Jean Dillinger ended his musings when she met him at the booth. She'd used her no-nonsense, straight-to-the-heart style to run his campaign since midsummer, and he appreciated her expertise. "Three hours here, possible run-over with the nice weather if the afternoon gets the expected turnout," she told him. "Which means not much more than a quick coffee between this and the Patriot dinner at the hotel. You're expected to give a five-minute address…"

"My favorite kind, short and sweet," he assured her, and she smiled.

"Short enough you can be off-the-cuff, and then a fifteen-minute question-and-answer period. Then dinner, where you will no doubt be approached by several people wanting you to support their causes, most of which are good solid things that'll allow you easy answers."

The Patriot Society had started small but now had over four hundred members and the support of many major local businesses. "I end the day with great food and nice people. Can't argue with that. But I will be glad when this is over, Jean."

She punched him on the arm. "Winning horses don't fade in the homestretch, Tug. This is a campaign, not a war, so muster up."

"I hate when you're right." He frowned at her. She responded with a knowing smile.

"Which is ninety-eight percent of the time. Folks are heading this way. Go get 'em, Sheriff."

The next time he checked his watch, over two hours had gone by.

He turned as a new group of people came his way, and when he recognized them, he grinned.

"Copper Guy!" Jeremy raced ahead of Christa and launched himself into Tug's arms. "We came to see you and get some apples and stuff. And they have a pony wagon, and Auntie Christa said we could go on it and take a ride and it goes around the whole town. Like this much!" He splayed his hands wide. "I have never been on a wagon ride in my whole life! And Nathan is coming, too, but Vangie was going to a friend's house, so it's just Nathan with us."

And then he flung his arms around Tug's neck and gave him the very best hug as Nathan and Christa drew closer.

He caught Christa's eye over the preschooler's shoulder. She'd tucked Jonah into a stroller, and looked the image of a happy young mother, despite the drama surrounding the small boy in front of her.

She smiled up at him, then began humming a song about heroes.

He didn't consider himself a hero. Just a good cop, doing his job, but he loved the boy's affection. He grinned back at her. "All in a day's work, ma'am."

"Then it was a very good day's work," she replied. "We thought it would be fun to come to the festival and see all the things."

"I'm stuck here or I'd happily wander around with you," he told her. He swept a quick look over the busy town park. "Three kids at a busy festival isn't a cakewalk."

"Did you just say that to an elementary schoolteacher who shepherds twenty-three children every day? Trust me, *Copper Guy.*" She rolled her eyes at his assertion. "This gig *is* a cakewalk."

"I stand corrected." His smile deepened. When other people began pressing in, he had to set Jeremy down. "I'll see you later, okay?"

"'Kay." Jeremy hugged him one more time. Then

Nathan hugged him, and he couldn't let them go without bending down to hug Jonah.

He wanted to hug Christa, too. He wanted the right to hug her in public, to hold her hand, to court her the way a woman should be wooed. How ironic that with all the cards, gifts and letters that had been inspired by Vangie's internet posting, God had put the right person here, in Golden Grove.

He couldn't help but smile at her. She must have read the intent in his eye because she took a firm step back with the stroller. "We'll let you get on with your day while we go take that wagon ride."

"Wish I could take it with you."

"Another time. And yes." She winked at him when no one could see. "That would be very nice."

The wink made him grin, and when he got to the more formal dinner two hours later, he couldn't get over the joy he'd felt at seeing her and the kids at the festival. It took effort to drive across the county, park at the school, maneuver kids, take the shuttle to the festival site, then repeat the process later.

She'd done it. And she'd brought Nathan along. As a single dad, he appreciated the work involved.

He walked into the dinner a happy man and stayed that way through his short address. Then the question-and-answer period came, and what had been a happy day changed after one question.

"Deputy, are you aware that your girlfriend had felony charges leveled against her in Sinclair, California, and if you are aware of this, how do you qualify your run for the sheriff's office by dating an ex-con?"

Tug stared at the man.

The hotel's conference room was filled to capacity. He heard the question, but couldn't believe he'd actually heard it at all. "Excuse me?"

"You're dating Christa Alero, is that correct?"

His heart beat a little louder and stronger in his chest. "Ms. Alero is a good friend of mine." The lameness of his answer surprised him, because Christa was more than a friend. At least he wanted her to be more than a friend. Way more. But he hadn't come to this dinner prepared to answer questions about her because it wasn't like they'd ever dated.

"And you're aware that your *friend*—" the man made quote marks with two fingers from each hand "—has a criminal record back in Sinclair?"

His mouth went dry.

His hands gripped the microphone tighter. Too tight, because the strong grip made his arm shake. His pulse spiked, making the whole thing almost surreal. "As a deputy sheriff, let me say that I make it a point not to delve into people's pasts beyond a certain point."

"So the idea of your girlfriend being an ex-con shouldn't be an issue for voters?"

He was blindsided, and it showed, and he knew at that moment that Converse's people wanted it to show. They'd planted someone here to ask the question, create last-minute negative headlines. But—and this was the hardest thing of all—they wouldn't have done this so blatantly and openly if there wasn't something to back it up. Something that Christa chose not to tell him. Something she'd kept hidden from him, and maybe from the school board, as well.

His throat was tight. His hands went numb.

He didn't let either physical reaction affect him. He turned the tables on the reporter. "What's your name, sir?"

"Don Malich."

"First, Mr. Malich, I'm not sure what you're referring to. I think that's obvious. Second, I'll be sure to check it out, but I have to wonder what lengths you went to in order to surprise me with this question?"

All eyes turned to Don Malich, and it was clear that the man hadn't expected to be put on the defensive. He'd figured this would go down the other way around, but Tug had been fighting crime for a long time. He understood his way around a football field…and an interrogation room. The best defense was an unshakable offense.

"Be assured that if any laws were broken, hedged or bent in order for you to become privy to this information, or anyone you're connected with, it will come back on you. And until I know more, that's all I have to say on that subject. Next question?"

Malich left quickly, scurrying out the upper door like a rabbit on the run. His actions almost said more than his words, but his words had said plenty. He'd been put in place as a device, but there was no way he wanted to be taken down with Converse's team.

Tug answered another ten minutes of questions.

He did it because he'd given his word, yet in the back of his mind, all he kept thinking of was Christa. The sadness. The regret he'd read as if it was old news. A regret he understood, but he'd never skated on the wrong side of the law.

Had she?

He went straight home after the dinner. He didn't

want to charge into her rental home in his current state of mind with accusations. He'd approach her in the morning, after church. But the next day, when he brought in the morning paper, there was a front-page article beneath a photo of him and Christa in the parking lot of the school beside her car. It had been taken on Friday, when he had his arm braced along her car behind her. He was looking down and she was gazing up at him with an expression that made his pulse quicken all over again.

Below the picture was a headline: Sheriff Candidate Dating Former Felon?

Renzo had warned him when the paper had come out with the article suggesting he'd put Vangie up to her video shenanigans. He'd hinted that the local paper was willing to play favorites and Tug had shrugged it off.

He should have listened because the timing of this couldn't be denied. Here was an article about him in the Sunday paper, the most read paper of the week in Grant County, with the election coming up on Tuesday.

And twenty-four hours after making mental plans for a happily-ever-after, he had to confront the woman he was falling in love with and find out what had happened in Sinclair.

Judging by the article, he wasn't going to like it.

Chapter Fourteen

Christa hurried the boys toward the white-spired church on Sunday morning. She crossed the street alongside the pharmacy, glanced down and stopped in her tracks when she spotted the bold-faced headline fronting the Sunday paper.

Sheriff Candidate Dating Former Felon?

She tried to swallow as realization broadsided her.

She couldn't because the secret she'd tried so hard to hide was laid out for everyone to see.

Her gut went tight as her heart sped up.

"Are we going in?" Jeremy tugged her hand toward the pretty church. They'd parked in the small municipal lot like so many others. Folks were passing them, hurrying up the walk, not wanting to be late for the service.

Should she go in and face people head-on or quietly walk away? Had they all read the paper this morning? And what exactly did it say?

Her chest clenched.

The chime of church bells began, a Golden Grove tradition seven days of the week. A sweet sound, beckoning folks to gather, but what would they think? What did they know?

She didn't want to buy the paper from the sidewalk box, but she didn't want to be in the dark, either. She slipped her card into the machine and it shuffled a paper into the basket below.

She couldn't read it here.

She tucked the paper under her arm and turned.

"We're not going?" Jeremy wasn't a big fan of sitting in church, but he whirled back toward the sidewalk. "I want to see my friend. We always see my friend here."

She wasn't sure if he meant Tug or Nathan, but it didn't matter. Gathering her wits was all that mattered at the moment, and then figuring out what to do. Two months ago, she'd been on top of the world. A new town, a new job, a place filled with hope.

The headline glared accusingly from another stand outside the small grocery as she crossed to the other side of the street.

Eyes down, she didn't look around as she took the boys back to the parking lot.

"Can't we just go like we're asposed to?" Jeremy begged. "You know we're asposed to go, Auntie Christa."

She couldn't bring herself to correct his speech. Or to answer, because if she did, she'd cry, and that would worry the boy needlessly.

She tucked Jonah into his car seat, then checked Jeremy's clasps once he'd buckled into his own.

She didn't want to think about the repercussions because she couldn't imagine them.

All she could see was the glare of that headline and the loss of what she'd worked so hard for. Multiple degrees, a good résumé, great recommendations and a solid job, right where she wanted to be. Now it would probably all come tumbling down around her.

You could have been honest from the beginning. Honesty is the best policy. What were you thinking?

She believed that, normally, but she'd also trusted a system that said her records were sealed.

Jubilee's words came back to her. How the official records were sealed, but that folks could examine old evidence and often put two and two together.

How could she face Tug?

Regret threatened to overtake her. She gripped the steering wheel with both hands, but it wasn't hard enough to calm the shaking.

"What's wrong?"

She glanced up, into the rearview mirror. Concerned big brown eyes met hers. "Does your tummy hurt, Auntie Christa?"

She nodded.

It wasn't a full-on lie because her gut *did* ache. Along with everything else.

She reached the house a few minutes later, and when the boys were busy playing with the interlocking blocks Darla had found in her attic, Christa pulled out the newspaper. She'd just read the article when her phone rang. Jubilee Samson's number appeared in the display. She seized the phone quickly. "You saw the paper."

"Just now. I came back from early service at my church and there it was. Christa, how did they get this? Has anyone interviewed you? Or asked you about it?"

"No," she replied, but then she remembered the missed call from yesterday morning. "Someone from the paper called yesterday but I couldn't take the call. I assumed they wanted me to subscribe or something. I never thought anything of it, but that must be why they said I didn't answer their calls."

Another shot of dismay coursed through her. Could she have prevented this if she'd answered the phone? Or would that have made things worse?

"They've put their own spin on it," noted Jubilee, "and the new owner of the paper has a different mind-set than most folks here, but this goes further than I would have expected."

"What does this mean for me and the boys? Or at least Jeremy, if Jonah's father takes him away," Christa whispered so the boys wouldn't overhear her side of the conversation. "Does this mean I'll lose Jeremy, too?"

Jubilee didn't offer false hope. "I can't predict how things will go, Christa, but they're pulling a rotten deal. It's clear they didn't get their hands on the sealed records, but they found enough people to talk and put the story together. This is horrible."

She'd already lost Marta and her mother. Now the ramifications of a stupid adolescent mistake could make her lose the boys.

"You sit tight and pray," Jubilee instructed her. "I know this looks dark, but that's often the case right before the dawn. I'll work on my end after the offices open up tomorrow and see what happens then. There's legal stuff and there's moral stuff, and between the two, I don't intend to lose Jeremy's chance at being with an aunt who loves him. I might not be able to promise the outcome, but I can promise you I won't leave a stone unturned to make sure we get the best possible chance at having a judge agree with us."

"Thank you, Jubilee. You're a voice of calm and reason and that's what I need right now."

"You stay quiet and don't let anybody intimidate you," Jubilee told her. "Sealed is sealed and they don't need to know anything else. For the moment, silence is golden."

Christa set down the phone, sure this couldn't get worse as Tug Moyer's SUV rolled into the driveway.

But from the grim expression on his normally kind, friendly face, she was pretty sure things had just gotten a whole lot worse.

Chapter Fifteen

Tug parked his SUV next to Christa's worn car. He'd looked for her in church, wondering what he could say. What he *should* say. Then he figured out why she wasn't there when a member of the congregation shoved the Sunday paper at him after the closing hymn. Now it wasn't a few hundred people at last night's dinner who knew what was going on. It was the whole county.

He walked toward the door.

She opened it before he got there, and stepped outside. The day was cool and a quick wind had risen midmorning. He paused by the side door, holding her gaze.

"You saw the paper."

"I didn't need to," he replied, and when she looked surprised, he went on. "I found out that I've become friends with a felon during the question-and-answer portion of the Patriot Club dinner last night."

Her jaw went slack and her pretty eyes filled with sorrow. "I'm sorry. Very sorry. It was a long time ago and I was told the records were sealed."

"They should be," he interrupted, but then he leaned

in. "If you were a juvenile when this occurred, then it's supposed to remain confidential for a reason. Kids don't make the best decisions. They mess up. Don't you get it, Christa?" He huffed out a breath and drew his hand through his hair, then across his neck in exasperation. "It's not about them finding out. It's about me not knowing."

"And being blindsided."

"No." He stared at her. She wasn't getting it. She raised her gaze to his and he wondered how they could see this so differently. "I don't care that you made mistakes as a kid. A lot of people do that and life goes on." He crossed his arms and braced his legs. "I care that you didn't trust me enough to *tell* me. That I didn't matter enough for you to be honest. That I had to hear it from some sanctimonious jerk last night and I had no idea how to defend you or our relationship because I didn't know I had to. I looked stupid and I don't like looking dumb or unprepared, but I can live with that." He paused again because this next part was the hardest thing to do. "What I can't live with is deceit. The lack of trust. You knowingly kept this from me while I was running for office. Were you ever going to tell me, Christa? Because when you're getting serious with a lawman, it might be in everyone's best interests for him to know that you've committed a felony."

Her shoulders straightened and her chin firmed. "Well, you know now. And if that's all you've got to say, then I need to get back in to the boys. I can't be leaving them on their own and it wouldn't look right to invite you inside. You never know who might be hanging around with a camera."

He didn't care about a camera. Or the article. He worked with kids all the time, and he understood their mess-ups better than most.

He cared about being betrayed. Being left out of the loop. He turned to leave, then swung back. "Were you ever going to tell me, Christa? Were you ever going to be honest with me?"

She held his gaze. Didn't flinch. And then she pointed one finger toward his SUV. "Please go." Then she pivoted, opened the door and went inside, quietly but firmly locking that heavy wooden door.

He wanted to scream and yell and let out all the frustration that had been building since last night's confrontation.

He didn't.

He strode toward that SUV even angrier than when he'd arrived. How had this happened? Why had it happened? And why had it happened to him after all the talk about God's perfect timing? What was perfect about discovering the woman you loved was a fraud? A liar.

He climbed into the driver's seat and shut the door a lot harder than he needed to.

He was too on edge to head home. It was the first weekend of November, the kids were at his mother's and—

Firewood.

He'd do what millions of men before him had done to calm their frayed nerves and explosive tempers. He'd cut firewood, and when he was done, he'd cut some more because it was going to take a whole lot of cutting and splitting to get through this. Fortunately, his father had kept a tract of forestland when he'd sold the orchard. It was quiet and filled with trees. The ideal place to go and be alone when you were about to lose something very near and dear to your heart.

Not the election.

There would always be more elections.

He was about to lose a woman he cared deeply about. A woman he loved, he realized as he drove north toward the forested areas. And not because she'd been a foolish kid, but because a relationship should be built on trust, and if she didn't trust him enough to be truthful, how could he trust her enough to be honest?

The last thing Christa wanted to do was face Darla and Glenn when she dropped the boys off on Monday morning, but there was no choice. What must they think of her?

That question jumbled her brain. She put a firm hold on her racing thoughts. She couldn't afford to let worry distract her in the classroom. She had a job to do, and she had every intention of doing her best as long as they kept her on.

"Hey." Darla hurried to the door when Christa approached their back steps with the boys. She took one look at Christa and swung the door wider. "I'm giving you fresh coffee, and no hug because I can see you're hanging on by a thread," declared the older woman. She leaned the door shut behind Christa. "But I will share some words of wisdom handed down by my grandmother—'and this too shall pass.' When she first laid that on me, I'd lost the man I loved. He'd been killed in Vietnam and I thought my life was over. It felt like it was, and for just a little while, I wanted it to be," said Darla as she fussed with the coffee system. "I was in such despair." She popped a pod in place, pressed a button and turned. "Then this apple farmer started delivering fresh fruit to the nursing home my father ran over in Quincy. He'd bring bushels of fruit with a smile, and every now and again he'd leave an apple or a pear on my desk. Even if I wasn't at my desk, he'd leave it there, right in the middle, just to make me smile. Later I found out he was scared I was going to starve myself to death, I'd gone so thin and gaunt. And he thought maybe a little fruit would tempt me to eat something. And it worked." She finished fixing Christa's coffee and handed it over. "Of course, it wasn't the fruit that made the difference. It was the patience. The steadfastness. That he would stop by my little billing office and leave samples of polished fruit he grew himself."

It wasn't a stretch to imagine the kind, quiet fruit farmer leaving a treat on Darla's desk, but Darla had done nothing wrong. "My case is quite different."

"It's not about blame," Darla insisted. "It's about timing and circumstances and faith. Stuff happens. We deal with it and move forward. Right now you have a lot to deal with and I'm sorry about that, but you did nothing wrong here, Christa. I blame dirty politics."

"If I hadn't messed up when I was fifteen, they'd have found nothing," she whispered. The boys had scrambled to the table where Darla had set triangles of warm French toast on their plates and she didn't want them to overhear. "I talked to Jubilee yesterday, and she's going to seek advice from her supervisors. Who knew that a stupid mistake back then would make such a difference now?"

"It shouldn't make any difference." Glenn came in from the dining room. He tipped his reading glasses up on his head and frowned. "Sealed should mean sealed and I don't have any respect for someone who goes out of their way to malign someone else. I've got a good mind to show up at the school board meeting tonight and tell them exactly what I think."

The biweekly school board meeting was scheduled for that night. Before tomorrow's election. And the moment Glenn mentioned that, Christa knew what she needed to do. "Can you guys watch the boys tonight?"

Darla nodded. "Of course. I'm home all evening." Then she put two and two together. "You're going to the meeting."

"Yes. I didn't listen to a lot of my mother's advice when I was young, but she taught me to face things head-on. Not to shrink back, and I'm going to do that tonight. I'll put myself on the list of speakers. Better to charge in on offense than play the whole game on defense."

"A football strategy I admire," said Glenn, and then he surprised her with a hug. "Let us therefore come boldly before the throne." He met her gaze calmly. "Paul was instructing the Hebrews to go forth boldly. It's a message that still works today."

She didn't want to do it.

That didn't matter.

She had to face this head-on because the thought of others talking carelessly about her wasn't just aggravating. It was wrong, and she was the only person who could set the record straight.

When she got to school, she messaged the secretary that she wanted to be put on the speakers' list for tonight's meeting. Then she planted a smile on her face and went into her classroom, determined to do her best. She couldn't control the newspaper or Tug's political opponent or the school board, but she could control what she brought to that classroom each day, and as long as she did that to the best of her ability, that was enough.

Chapter Sixteen

Seventeen kids showed up to shoot hoops on Monday afternoon.

Renzo walked into the gym, spotted the turnout and whistled softly. "This is double what we've been getting. That's a nice change."

"Agreed."

"Split into two?"

The gym was big enough for two small courts or one large one. "Yes. And then let's do some of our old drills halfway through."

"Get them ready for next year's tryouts."

"That's the hope," Tug answered softly.

Renzo divided the groups up for a scrimmage, and when Tug re-formed the kids into drill lines for the last thirty minutes, a few complained.

But most listened.

Tillie had kept score for the scrimmages, but now she surprised him by getting into line for the drills. "Hey." He grinned and checked the ball to her.

She caught it and nailed him with a quick and accurate chest pass. "They're having a girls' team, too. I figured, why not?"

"I like how you think," he told her, then wondered if his mother might be able to watch Tillie's little brother so Tillie could practice.

By the time the drills were done, the kids had to scramble to catch the late buses home. He grabbed a towel, slung it over his neck and glanced at the clock. Christa would be picking up the boys in about fifteen minutes. He'd stay at school to purposely avoid the confrontation. He fist-bumped Renzo and headed toward his office.

"You're not going home?"

"Soon. Paperwork calls."

"You avoiding Christa?"

A thread of displeasure crept up Tug's neck. "That's not open for conversation, Renzo."

A basketball whizzed by his head. He turned swiftly as the ball careened off the closed bleachers. "What was that for?"

"To get your attention because you're being stupid. Are you seriously ditching a wonderful woman because she messed up almost fifteen years ago?" Renzo came closer. "You? The guy who works with kids all the time, the guy who hands out second chances like popcorn at the movies?"

Tug retrieved the ball and kept walking.

"So that's it?"

He tucked the ball beneath his arm and turned. "Renzo, we've been friends all our lives, but this is different. You can't help on this one and I can't fix it. It's not about what she did back then. It's about keeping it a secret from me.

How can I trust someone who doesn't trust me enough to be honest?"

Renzo's brows shot up in disbelief. "You've known her for seven weeks. Is that supposed to be enough time for her to blurt out her life story? With you running for sheriff and her in a new job and then suddenly guardian to two little boys, one of them about to be wrenched away by the courts. Yeah, I can see why you'd be upset because she didn't manage to fit in fifteen years of explanation into that scenario. It's not as if she came here for a normal job only to end up losing family and gaining two kids. My bad."

Renzo didn't stick around to hear Tug's answer. He crossed the gym and the soft click of the outside door said he'd left the building.

Tug put the ball away and started walking back to his middle-school office.

Renzo was right.

He hated that.

He'd been thinking along those same lines all day, but each time he went to pick up the phone or stop by Christa's room, he stopped himself because honesty mattered. It mattered a lot, and he couldn't work his anger around an excuse, but Renzo's argument made sense. It wasn't as if they'd had time for heart-to-hearts about anything. Their lives had been twisted around jobs and kids, the coming election and moving Christa and the boys into the O'Laughlin house. Thinking back, he didn't know many women who could have done half of that with Christa's panache.

"See ya tomorrow!" Tillie had grabbed a couple of books from her locker and was trying to shove them into her worn backpack as she rushed past him to catch the bus. "Thanks for practicing with me!"

"Anytime, kid."

A handful of marching band members joined her inside the exit door. When he saw the small group chatting, it touched his heart. Tillie wouldn't have talked to those kids a few weeks ago. She wouldn't have stayed late, or changed her schedule to get home to Alfie and stay up later to do her homework. She'd shown him a B on two papers the previous Friday and there was no mistaking the pride in her eyes.

He gathered his things and headed to his mother's, but when he got there, Jeremy and Jonah were happily eating cheese pizza at the table. "Christa didn't come for the boys?" he asked as he came into the room.

"Later," Darla told him. "She's addressing the school board tonight and needed some time to get ready, so I'm keeping the boys here."

"Addressing the school board?" He'd been reaching for the coffeepot on the counter. He stopped. "About the article in the paper?"

"She said she wants to face it head-on," Darla told him. "Gutsy move."

It was. The article had been primarily hearsay and innuendo, told through the eyes of old neighbors or classmates because the official records *were* closed to the public, but it had enough fact to make people assume that they'd hired a former felon to teach their young. "She doesn't have to do that."

"Maybe she does." His mother handed the boys each a juice pouch and turned. "If *everyone* reacts badly to that article—"

Like he had. She didn't say it but he read the implication in her tone.

"—then she has to live her life dodging gossip and misconceptions. Better they hear it from the source rather than make up their own stories behind the scenes."

"Is Christa in trouble?" Vangie came into the kitchen and crossed her arms in a move that reflected his.

"No, of course not," he told her, but would they pressure her to leave? He really had no idea. "Mom, are you okay if my two hang out here also?"

"The more the merrier," she told him. "You want a sandwich before you go?"

"I'll get one later." He'd have just enough time to get to the meeting if he left right now.

He pulled into the Golden Grove Schools central office parking area a few minutes after the meeting began. He slipped into the back of the room and scanned the seats.

He spotted Christa at once. She was right up front, her hair pulled back into a bun, chin up, face calm as she listened to the board attend to normal business. Tonight, this was a typical meeting room. Tomorrow, it would be used for voting in the general election. Her fate was being challenged tonight. His would be decided tomorrow. The irony that the two situations would take place in the same room wasn't lost on him.

It was nearly seven o'clock before the board completed their last scheduled discussion. The board president called Christa's name and the room watched as she moved to the public microphone. She set a paper onto the lectern and folded her hands, but not before Tug noticed the slight tremble of her fingers.

Sympathy swept him. He tamped it down because honesty wasn't too much to ask, was it? But Renzo's words sparked truth, too. Maybe he was expecting too much in the short time they'd had together.

He stopped thinking about it when she addressed the board. "I've come to apologize to the board and to this community," she began. "Someone has been digging into my past, and if you've read the article in the *Sunday Chronicle*, you've seen what they hinted at about me. I am here to tell you that each and every word you read is sadly true."

Not one person on that board moved a muscle. They sat as one, watching. Listening. Just like him, and hearing Christa recount sordid details from her past for the next ten minutes, he got a real clear image of what her life had been like then.

Yet here she was. A teaching professional who sought a life dedicated to helping children from all walks of life attain the education she'd worked hard to secure for herself.

"I pleaded guilty because I felt guilty," she finished, after offering the horrific details of the night in question. "The public defender assured me that was the best way to go." She paused, then explained the situation. "I was fifteen and I'd greatly disappointed my hardworking mother. If we'd had better advice about the legal system, or money for a better lawyer, it would have been handled differently and probably none of us would be here now because there would be no sealed records to talk about. But poor kids don't generally get those choices. I'm not saying that for sympathy," she assured them. "It's simply a fact.

"I did my community service, finished school and went on to college. A professor there used an example of how difficult it can be for a white teacher to earn the trust of a minority classroom. Not because of the teacher's lack, but because those children sitting there might not be able to fully relate. That's when I decided to become a teacher.

"My mother never got to see me graduate. She died my junior year of college. But if she can see me now, I hope she's proud. And on a final note, I didn't mean to lie to the board or the selection committee." She added this with an aside to a high-school teacher on her left, a man who served on the interview committee.

"Sealed records are supposed to be kept secret and I never dreamed it would come to light. I apologize if that seems dishonest in any way. I can assure you it wasn't meant to be and that's what brought me here tonight. It's better to be known for the truth than maligned for half-truths. If you have any questions for me, I'll do my best to answer them at this time."

Just as she began answering questions, his phone buzzed.

Got to see you. Meet me at Walker and Park.

Renzo never asked for something like this unless it was critical. Tug texted back. On my way.

He wanted to stay and talk to Christa.

He couldn't, and he left that room feeling like a jerk for his quick reaction the previous day. He needed to talk with her, ask for her forgiveness, because a man who prided himself on helping teens find a righteous path should have had more empathy for her history.

He'd fix it. Somehow, someway, he'd fix what he'd messed up because she deserved someone who would stand beside her in thick and thin, and he wanted to be that someone.

He pulled into a parking spot on Park Road and got out of his car. Renzo's truck was two spots up. He came Tug's way, looked around to make sure they were alone and handed over a picture of Danny Adams.

Tug looked at the picture, then Renzo. "What's this for? I know who Danny Adams is."

"Meet Mark Adams, Danny's identical twin brother," said Renzo. "And Mark has things to tell you. First thing tomorrow, we're going to the drug treatment center in Ellensburg to meet him, because Mark told me that Danny isn't Jonah's father. He is. And he says he'll swear to it in a court of law because Danny doesn't want Jonah to raise as his own."

"So Danny's his uncle?" Tug frowned. "He's still family and the judge might still go that way."

Renzo's expression went hard and flat as he continued. "Mark told me that Danny doesn't want Jonah for himself. When I explained the situation, he said Danny is trying to fulfill an arrangement he had with Marta before she died. An arrangement to hand Jonah over to a barren Louisiana couple for a very large sum of money, a deal that was arranged several months ago. A deal that Danny Adams is trying to close by pretending to be Jonah's father."

Tug's gut twisted. The thought that anyone could be

that heartless and greedy wasn't just appalling. It was sickening. "How'd you find this out?"

"Things weren't adding up," Renzo replied.

Tug understood because he'd felt the same way.

"So I dug further, and when I turned up a brother who was here, in rehab, I wanted to talk to him. Imagine my surprise when I walked into the house and there was the exact image of Danny Adams sitting at the kitchen table."

"He's sure he's the father?"

"Absolutely certain. His brother wasn't even in the area nine months before Jonah was born. And that's another thing," Renzo told him. "The boys' birthdays were altered to make them seem younger. Younger children bring a higher price on the black market, so they shaved six months off their birthdays and paid to have new birth certificates made up. I double-checked that at county records and the real records show that Jeremy will be five in two weeks and Jonah turned three in June."

"And the mother was part of this ruse?"

Renzo nodded. "She told him she knew she wasn't good for the boys, and she didn't want them turned over to social services or foster care, and that if people were willing to pay tens of thousands of dollars for a child, they must be rich enough to give them a good life."

The desperation of addiction was an ugly thing and he'd seen people willing to do almost anything to secure that next hit. The temptation of all that money plus a safe place for her children had ended in drastic results. Was Marta's death involved in this scheme? He didn't know, but he'd make sure their detective bureau would begin an investigation right away.

"I don't know how to thank you, man." He hugged Renzo. His friend had gone the distance.

"None needed. Nothing was adding up. I sat in church yesterday morning and turned it over to God because I felt like I was missing the obvious. And as I was walking out of church, it came to me to roll the case backward. When I delved into Danny's past, it didn't link to any kind of family, and who doesn't link to some kind of family these days? That sent up a red flag. And now we know. Our computer expert managed to fly under the radar and remove traces of family from typical internet searches. If nothing else, this should help Christa breathe easier because Jonah's real father simply wants what's best for his son but he also recognizes his frailty because this is his third time in rehab. He wants to relinquish his parental rights and name Christa as Jonah's guardian. And he said he won't oppose an adoption if she decides to take that route."

A huge weight lifted from Tug's shoulders.

He'd thought that tomorrow's election was a big deal.

It wasn't compared to this. Whatever happened with the election results, he would still be doing the job he loved. But being able to give Christa this news meant everything. Her well-being and peace of mind ranked higher than his goals and his career. He wanted to rush right over there and tell her now, but that could set her up for another fall if this didn't work out. He and Renzo would meet with Mark Adams tomorrow. And then he'd inform Christa and Jubilee of what they'd discovered.

"I'll see you in the morning." Renzo gave him a

light punch on the arm. "It's a great way to start your big day."

Funny. The election had just taken second place behind Renzo's discovery. "Tomorrow's outcome has nothing on the news you just gave me. Knowing Christa can keep Jonah and Jeremy together isn't just good news. It's the best news ever. You did great, partner."

"Just trying to get in good with the new sheriff." Renzo winked and moved toward his car.

Tomorrow's election was important, yes. He was the best man for the job. Tug believed that. But if it didn't happen, that was all right because he loved what he did right now, too. And he meant what he'd said to his longtime partner, that the news about Jonah's father ranked first.

Because when it came right down to it, weren't kids the most important thing of all?

Chapter Seventeen

Christa dropped the boys at Darla's the next morning and headed to school. A much-needed good night's sleep had refreshed her and the short drive gave her time to reflect on the evening before.

She'd done it.

She'd been scared at first, but the board members treated her with dignity throughout the evening. That was huge.

But when Tug left without talking to her, she'd had to re-paste a look of calm on her face.

She'd done well. But not well enough to appease Tug's disappointment in her. He'd been making it a habit to greet kids as they arrived at school each morning. With staggered start times he'd go from school to school, high-fiving and shaking hands as kids streamed through the doors.

There was no sign of him today. Was he hiding away, anxiously awaiting election results? Hoping her past didn't ruin his goals for the future?

She wouldn't blame him if that were the case, but

she'd come clean and now the rest was up to Golden Grove schools.

She went through the day with her chin up, but she checked her phone twice to see if there were any polling numbers on the local stations.

Nothing.

She finished the day and crossed the school grounds to the central office wing of the middle school where a vote-here sign pointed to the same room she'd been in the night before. She went in, got her name checked off the registry and cast her ballot. And when an elections volunteer gave her an I-voted-today sticker to wear, she peeled off the paper backing and put it on her collar.

Then she went to pick up the boys.

Would Tug be at his parents' house?

Probably not, and she wasn't sure if that was good or bad. A part of her wanted to confront him. Scold him for being closed-minded.

Another part wanted to apologize for keeping her past a secret once they became attracted to one another. She could have opened up then, and she hadn't. Her fault, totally.

"I didn't even see Copper Guy one time today." Jeremy folded his little arms once they got back to their rental house and scowled. "You know how he picks me up and turns me upside down? And then I laugh at him and he laughs at me?"

The image made Christa long for more of those sweet moments. "I do. And I'm sure he'll do that again. He was busy today."

"Well, I'm busy every day, but I still like to see him," Jeremy protested. "Right, Jonah?"

"Jemmie, I miss him so much!" Always earnest, Jonah added a cute, pleading expression that tipped Christa into overdrive.

"Guys, it's been one day. That's really not all that long," she reminded them. "I promise you'll see Tug soon."

Jeremy grumbled as he scowled at the bathtub. "Why do we have to take a dumb bath? Because I don't even want to do that."

"Gotta be clean, kid."

"I'll just get dirty again tomorrow," he declared, but he climbed into the tub and plunked himself down. Two minutes later, he'd forgotten the drama and was having fun racing sharks and dinosaurs around his little brother when the doorbell rang.

She eyed the boys and the stairs. She couldn't leave them alone in the tub. But the doorbell rang again. When she didn't answer, a text came up on her phone. Can I come in?

Tug.

Her pulse hiked instantly and she may have caught her breath, but then common sense took over. Giving the boys a bath, sorry.

I'm good at bathing kids, he texted back. And I got an A in bedtime stories 101.

He was being charming.

She loved that about him. Truthfully, there wasn't a thing she didn't love about him, but could he forgive her sin of omission? More to the point, *should* he? And it wasn't as if she was all too pleased with him at the moment, either. Life hadn't exactly been a walk in the park for her, but she'd overcome, and no matter what happened, she'd give herself a firm pat on the back for that. Don't you have election results to watch? she texted.

In two hours. Plenty of time.

Mixed emotions flooded her, but she typed Come in quickly because she knew seeing Tug would make the boys' day. When the big guy strolled into the upstairs bathroom a minute later, Jeremy's joy confirmed her decision.

"Copper Guy!"

"Hey, dude, I thought I'd stop around for bath time and story time. Whaddya say?" He fist-bumped each boy and the adorable little traitors grinned up at him as if their best dreams had all come true. "Anybody ready to get out?"

"We bofe are." Jonah stood quickly. He almost tumbled but Christa grabbed hold of his slippery arm and kept him from falling. Then she gathered him into a soft old towel. "You smell amazing," she told him, and she nuzzled his wet little neck.

"That tickles!" He giggled and shrieked as Jeremy scrambled out of the tub for time with his hero.

"He's a baby." Jeremy indicated Jonah with a wave of his hand. "Big guys aren't ticklish, like not even a little."

"No?" Tug proved him wrong by blowing raspberry kisses to his neck until he laughed out loud, just like his brother.

"I thought I was too big for those things!" he exclaimed as Tug wrapped him into a second towel. "Do it again!"

"One more, then pajamas."

"Okay!" he said, and when he was finally done giggling at Tug's antics, he hugged Tug's neck. "I'm so glad you came over. I was missing you so much and I was even mad."

"Mad at who?" asked Tug as Jeremy slipped into comfy pajama pants and a long-sleeved tee.

"At everybody because you didn't even come see us once today."

"And now I did," Tug offered sensibly.

"I know, so that's good, right?" Jeremy scrambled into his arms again. "Because friends should always be together. Because they love each other and they want to, that's why."

Tug lifted that heartfelt gaze to her. "Because they love each other and they want to."

Her head knew he was simply repeating the boy's words, but that didn't stop her heart from racing. She covered by heading downstairs. "You can each pick out two stories."

"I know 'zacly which ones I'm picking." Jeremy had two favorites and he rarely went outside his comfort zone. Jonah was always looking for new stories, even with their somewhat thin selection. He liked things to differ. Brothers, alike in some ways, different in others. They might differ in traits, but the love they shared was sweet and sincere.

"I'll read first," said Tug as he settled into a corner of the couch.

Christa took the chair opposite.

Jeremy had been snuggling in next to Tug, but when she sat over there, he straightened in surprise. "Aren't you going to sit with us?"

"I can listen just fine from here." She patted the chair arm and smiled.

"'Cept you can't see the pictures," Jeremy reminded her. "And remember how you said they made really nice pictures to go with the story so people can see the story and listen to the story."

"I did say that, but I know what the pictures look like because we've read this book dozens of times. You enjoy your time with Copper Guy. Remember how you were missing him?" No way was she about to snuggle next to Tug as if everything were all right, because it wasn't. And yet she was grateful that he'd taken the time to come see the boys, and on a critical day for him, too. That kindness wasn't lost on her.

By the time the four stories were completed, Jeremy was yawning and Jonah was semi-dozing. So sweet. So very special.

Jeremy grabbed a stuffed bear Darla had given him and walked upstairs while Tug carried Jonah. He tucked the boys in, kissed them good-night and stepped aside so Christa could do the same.

The past few weeks she'd loved this. Two adults, sharing moments, getting to know one another and having fun with the kids. She'd never dreamed of wealth or glamour growing up.

She'd dreamed of normal.

This kind of normal.

But normal carried its own kind of heartbreak and she'd have to be strong enough to handle whatever came her way. With faith, she'd do just that.

Tug preceded her downstairs, and when he got to the bottom, he motioned to the couch. "I've got some good news for you. Can we talk?"

She wanted to say yes, because she wanted the election to go well for him, but they didn't have to share a couch to do that. "You're leading in the polls?"

"I promised myself not to look or listen until the results come in, so I have no idea," he replied. Then he took a seat on the couch and motioned to a folder on the side table. "This is more important and I think it's going to make you very happy. It's about Jonah."

She moved his way and took a seat. "What about Jonah?"

He opened the folder and slipped out three pieces of paper. There were two pictures of Danny Adams and one official-looking signed paper. "Did the judge render a decision?" she asked, puzzled.

"The petition has been dropped," he told her. "Because this man—" he pointed to one picture "—is Danny Adams and Danny isn't Jonah's father."

"But the testing showed that he was." This wasn't making sense. She understood the accuracy of the testing. She'd searched the internet, hoping to find a flaw, but the tests were very reliable.

"This is Mark Adams." Tug handed her the next picture. "Danny's identical twin. He is Jonah's father. When Renzo couldn't find any family links to Danny Adams on the web, he dug deeper and discovered Mark's existence. And when he found Mark in a rehab program in Ellensburg, he contacted him and Mark confirmed that he and Marta had a relationship nine months before Jonah was born. I went to see him this morning."

"That's why you weren't at the school."

He paused and gave her that crooked smile. The one that set her heart to racing. "You missed me?" he asked.

"I noticed," she corrected him. "What did Mark

Adams say? Why would his brother claim paternity for a nephew? Was he trying to save Jonah for his brother?" He'd said this was good news, but how could finding another relative, the boy's true father, make things better? She was pretty sure that only made things twice as bad, but then Tug reached out.

Took her hand.

And something about the look on his strong, kind face made her almost think everything could be all right, after all.

...

Chapter Eighteen

Tug firmed his jaw and shook his head. "Nothing that gallant. It seems that he'd been helping Marta set up a paid adoption of the boys and Jonah's was scheduled to go through at the same time Marta disappeared and the boys went off the grid."

Christa's gaze sharpened. "You can't be serious. She was selling her children?"

There was no way to soft-peddle this kind of truth. "She knew she wasn't good for them and she wanted to reestablish her life. Danny had new birth certificates made for the boys, shaving six months off their birthdays. Jonah's new parents were supposed to pick him up in September, and when the boy wasn't delivered, they were upset. Danny explained that with the mother deceased, he needed to establish paternity to complete the transaction."

"I can't believe this." Christa put her face in her hands, trying to make sense of what she was hearing. "What kind of person does something like this? Who tries to sell their own flesh and blood?"

Tug had been a cop for a decade and a half. He'd seen a lot of wretched situations. "Desperate people do desperate things."

"I was so angry when my mother made Marta leave because I loved her. She was like a sister to me, and I didn't trust my mother's judgment. Clearly she was right all along and I made Mom's life miserable because I was so angry. I can't defend my actions then, and I certainly can't defend Marta's now. So what does this mean, Tug? For Jonah? The courts won't give him to his uncle, will they?"

"Absolutely not," he assured her. "This is from Mark Adams, a writ of release asking the courts to give you full rights of guardianship and adoption if you so choose."

She stared at him. Her eyes went wide. Then they filled with tears as she looked to the paper, then him again. "I get to keep him?"

"Yes."

"Oh, Tug." She hugged him then. Hugged him tight, and that gesture opened a window of hope within him. "I don't know how to thank you."

"It was all Renzo," he told her, but he didn't refuse the hug. In fact, he drew her closer and wrapped his arms around her. "I had to stay away from the investigation because I had a conflict of interest, but Renzo followed through one hundred percent. *He* should be getting the hug," he went on. "But I'm happy to stand in for him."

She started to pull back.

He didn't let her. He put his lips against her soft hair and whispered, "So can we talk about us now?"

She did pull back then. "There is no us," she told him.

She swiped happy tears from her cheeks with the backs of her hands until he reached around her to the tissue box and grabbed a handful. He thrust them at her. "These work better. And why isn't there an us? Because I acted like a jerk? Because I jumped to conclusions and didn't give you a chance to explain?"

"All of the above?" she countered. She wiped her eyes and nose before she went on, and even with tear-filled eyes, she was absolutely downright beautiful. "I'm sorry I wasn't up-front with you about my past, but it's not exactly the first thing you blurt out to people," she scolded with more of her usual sass. "But I should have told you, because when you have feelings for someone—"

"I do like the sound of that," he whispered and managed to nuzzle her ear softly. "Because I've got some pretty strong feelings myself, darling."

"So now I'm your darling?" She wasn't giving him much slack, but that was his fault. Not hers.

"You were always my darling. I should have chopped wood before I came to see you. It was a stupid decision I will never make again. So…" He set his forehead against hers lightly. Her breath mingled with his. Her hair—her dark pretty hair—smelled of little kid soap and sweet apples. A perfect scent for a Washington November. "Let's fix it. I'm sorry I reacted badly and stomped off. I was wrong to do that."

She pulled back slightly so he could meet her gaze. Search those beautiful dark brown eyes. "You had every right to be upset."

"I did." His quick agreement made her frown reappear. Possibly deeper than it had been. "But a just man reasons things out, and the minute I walked away I thought about all the kids I talk with on the internet. The mistakes they make, the choices that get them into and out of trouble. And I realized that if I found it so easy to encourage and forgive children I don't even know, how could I justify my reaction to your story?"

"It was justified because I should have told you," she answered softly.

"Those were my thoughts," he admitted, "but then someone reminded me that we'd only known each other for seven weeks, and that most couples don't bare their souls in that length of time. He also mentioned that I was stupid."

"Renzo."

"Good old Renzo. So here it is." He straightened and faced her. "I want to get to know you. To court you. To spend time with you and the boys and have you spend more time with Nathan and Evangeline. This whole thing started with Vangie's quest for a wife for me. Vangie meant well, but kids don't see the whole picture. It's not just about romance when you're a single parent, although I might add I feel ridiculously romantic whenever I'm near you." He kissed her cheek gently. "Or hear your voice." Now his lips kissed the other cheek. "Or just think about you at any place, at any time of day. So we've got that part covered." He lowered his mouth to hers and kissed her, then pulled back. He sighed. "It's about family, and stepping into a stepparent role isn't easy. She thinks I haven't dated because I don't make time for it. She's wrong," he went on. "I haven't dated because I can't risk messing up my kids any more than I already have."

"Your kids are amazing. They are not messed up at all," she corrected him.

"Hadley died of ovarian cancer," he told her. "She'd had weird symptoms for nearly a year. We were busy and she brushed the discomforts off as if they were no big deal, and I let her do it. And even when she went to the doctor, they gave her meds for a troubled stomach and left it at that. If I had pushed harder, if I hadn't been so busy with work and helping kids, maybe we could have gotten her in for treatment sooner. But I didn't push, and when she was gone, it was like this layer of guilt just descended over me."

"Guilt is a tough thing to handle. But if we start blaming ourselves for things that are out of our control, then who are we helping?" she asked. "No one."

"My father reminded me of that. He said no matter how strong you think you are, God's timing takes precedence. And he was right." He tugged her back into the curve of his arm, tucked against his shoulder and his chest. "So can we try this again? I want a chance to convince the most wonderful woman in the world that I won't ever be a jerk again. Because that would make me real happy right now."

"Even if you don't win the election?" she asked, teasing.

He smiled against her hair, then wrapped her in a hug. A hug that felt so good he didn't want to let go. Ever. But he did. "Even if. I should head over to the offices. I'm meeting Mom and Dad and the kids there. Just in case." He kissed her one more time, then stood up.

"And if we win, let's have a family celebration dinner on Friday night. All eight of us. We could go to someplace fancy—"

"Or we order Chinese and play games at your parents' house," she cut in.

"And then we get a babysitter and go out on our own on Saturday night," he suggested. "Like a date. A real one. Just you and me." And when she smiled and leaned up for another kiss, he knew he'd made his point. "Gotta go."

She reached for the TV remote. "I'll be watching."

"And I'll text you the minute I know."

She hugged him and watched him go out the door.

He trotted to his car, and when he swung it around, there she was, waving from the side door.

No matter what the rest of the night brought, he could already count today as a success. Jonah and Jeremy would be safe and beloved in Christa's care and he'd managed to fall in love again—for the last time in his life.

Sure, a victory would top things off, but he'd learned a hard lesson years before. Life wasn't about winning or losing. It was about loving and learning, and he'd done his share of that.

Epilogue

"How are we doing with the party stuff, my love?"
Christa looked up at Tug as she began marking off a
checklist the following August.

"Water balloons are filled and ready, helium balloons
are hung on the mailbox and every possible place you
can imagine."

She laughed as a soft breeze sent the balloons bob-
bing and weaving around her. "It looks perfect! And the
coolers are filled with ice and juice boxes?"

"Yes and yes. And when Renzo and I finish this
banner, we'll run the streamers from the garage to the
house like we planned." Tug stretched to affix the top
and bottom tie-downs of the big banner while Renzo
held the far side of the banner steady. "I'm set here,"
he told Renzo. "Wait for the boss to make sure we've
got this right," he added with a grin down to his wife.

Christa didn't take the bait. She moved across the
driveway, then gave them a firm thumbs-up. "It's perfect. I want the boys to get here and be absolutely over

the moon to see this Adoption Day party is all about them."

Vangie was helping Glenn set up chairs. "What time do we have to be in court?" she asked.

"Ninety minutes. Just enough time to make this yard a celebration of love," Christa told her. "And I'm so glad to have your help, Vangie."

"Grandma's got the tough job," Vangie replied as she moved a folding table into place with her grandfather. "Keeping three boys clean before we meet with the judge. Helping Gramps is super easy compared to that."

"There's significant truth to her words," muttered Tug from the ladder. Then he paused and smiled down at Christa. "Are you as excited as I am?"

"I felt like this day would never come, and now that it has, I keep wondering if I'm good enough to be their mom," she confessed in a softer voice. "But then I realize they're going to have a really cool sheriff for a dad—"

Renzo snorted as Tug puffed out his chest. "I'm pretty sure their job will be to keep you humble," Renzo reminded him.

"Says the guy helping his mother with triplets," Tug shot back. "Are you helping her get the girls over here for the party?"

"Me, who's never worried about a car seat in the back of my muscle car, now have two installed, so the answer is yes. And this is the reason our mothers get along so well," he continued with a well-placed sigh. "They're not afraid to tackle things. Mostly because they know we can be shamed into helping as needed."

Christa laughed. "I don't expect there's a lot of shaming going on. But three preschoolers on a cattle farm is a lot, isn't it?"

"Shift work," Renzo told her as he climbed down the ladder. He lifted it and began moving toward the garage. "It's all in the scheduling, according to my mother."

By the time the yard was set they had just a half hour to get changed and make it to the courthouse.

Darla and the three boys were waiting in the air-conditioned entry when they arrived.

All three raced for Christa and Tug. Nathan, such a funny, sincere little boy who'd lost his beloved mother too soon, and Jeremy and Jonah, two abandoned children who would never be cast off again.

"Can't we just be like always?" Jeremy asked as Tug lifted him into his arms. "Do we have to go in there and see this guy again?"

"This guy is a judge and he's very nice," Christa reminded him. "And, yes, if we want this adoption to proceed, we have to do exactly that. Let's go see what he has to say, okay?" She sprinkled kisses on Jeremy's cheeks until he laughed, and when the judge's door opened, she took a deep breath.

"We've got this." Tug bent slightly to whisper the soft encouragement into her ear. "No worries. When God is with us, who can be against us?"

His words helped. Having him by her side helped even more. They weren't entering this new normal with blinders on. They were moving forward with faith, hope and love, just the way she prayed it would be.

The judge gave his approval a quarter hour later and officially signed Jonah and Jeremy over to Terrence and Christa Moyer.

He shook their hands. Then he posed for Adoption Day pictures and even hugged the boys. And when they pulled into the driveway of Tug's home—their home now—the boys' eyes grew wide.

"Is this a party?" Jeremy sought Christa's hand, and when he grabbed hold, he held on tight. "Like a birthday party?"

"It's the birthday of our new family," Christa told him.

Jonah didn't hold back. He whooped and hollered and dashed for one of the bouncy houses Renzo had set up in the backyard. He was all boy, in his element, loving life.

Jeremy lifted his more cautious gaze to Christa and Tug. "There are presents."

"For you and Jonah," Tug replied. He squatted low. "We're celebrating being a family because today that judge made it official. Auntie Christa will be your mom. And I get to be your dad, just like we talked about. Okay?"

"Do I have to call you Mom?"

An old ache touched Christa's heart. "You can call me whatever you want, Jeremy. It's fine."

"It's just... I still miss my mom." He looked embarrassed to admit that, as if he shouldn't love his late mother. "Just a little."

Tug reached out and hugged the boy. "When our moms go to Heaven we always miss them, honey. But God says it's okay to love other people, too. He made our hearts extra big that way."

"Jemmie! Look how high I can jump! I'm like an astronaut guy," Jonah squealed as he and five or six other kids rocked the red, yellow and blue bouncy castle.

Jeremy turned to look. His brother's joy seemed to ease his concerns. "I'm coming, Jonah! We can be astronauts together!"

He raced off as Tug slipped an arm around Christa's shoulders. "He'll be fine, honey."

"I know. It's just hard to think of all these guys have been through." She leaned against him as friends put out refreshments while others organized a table laden with gifts. "So now I won't think of that," she told him. "I'm going to focus on our future. Not the past. And if God were to hold a little surprise in our future for next spring, what would my beloved husband say?"

Tug pulled her into one of the hugs she loved so much. He held her there and dropped his mouth to her ear. "He'd say he's the most blessed man on the face of the earth. And that he better have someone get going on that addition we talked about." He pulled back just enough to kiss her. "Because it seems like we're going to be needing it real soon. And I couldn't be happier, wife."

She kissed him back, then turned slightly to see the kids all running, bouncing and having the time of their lives. "Me, either."

* * * * *

*If you loved this story,
be sure to pick up the first book in
Ruth Logan Herne's Golden Grove miniseries
A Hopeful Harvest*

*And check out the titles from her previous series
Shepherd's Crossing*

*Her Cowboy Reunion
A Cowboy in Shepherd's Crossing
Healing the Cowboy's Heart*

Available now from Love Inspired!

Find more great reads at www.LoveInspired.com

Dear Reader,

Oh, how I loved writing this story. Having grown up poor, I know the downsides of being marginalized, but I'm also a big fan of teachers and cops that go the extra distance for kids and that's why I picked two such wonderful champions for this story. For Tug and Christa, God's perfect timing was put to the test and emerged triumphant.

Grown-ups have such influence on kids. We don't always see it, and we don't necessarily witness the fruits of our labors, but that love and support for kids of all ages can make a huge difference. Kindness and truthfulness and busy hands are a perfect combination!

I love to hear from readers. It's like my favorite thing! Feel free to email me at loganherne@gmail.com, friend me on Facebook, visit my website, ruthloganherne.com, or swing by the Yankee-Belle Café at yankeebellecafe.blogspot.com to chat with authors there about life, love and food! And thank you so much for reading this beautiful story!

With love,
Ruthy

SPECIAL EXCERPT FROM

🌿

LOVE INSPIRED
INSPIRATIONAL ROMANCE

Intent on reopening a local bed-and-breakfast,
Addie Ricci sank all her savings into the project—and
now the single mother's in over her head. But her high
school sweetheart's back in town and happy to lend a
hand. Will Addie's long-kept secret stand in the way of
their second chance?

Read on for a sneak preview of
Her Hidden Hope *by Jill Lynn,*
part of her Colorado Grooms *miniseries.*

Addie kept monopolizing Evan's time. First at the B and B—though she could hardly blame herself for that. He was the one who'd insisted on helping her out. And now again at church. Surely he had better places to be than with her.

"Do you need to go?" she asked Evan. "Sorry I kept you so long."

"I'm not in a rush. I might pop out to Wilder Ranch for lunch with Jace and Mackenzie. After that I have to…" Evan groaned.

"Run into a burning building? Perform brain surgery? Teach a sewing class?"

Humor momentarily flashed across his features. "Go to a meeting for Old Westbend Weekend."

What? So much for some Evan-free time to pull herself back together. "I'm going to that, but I didn't realize you were. The B and B is one of the sponsors for the weekend." Addie had used her entire limited advertising budget for the three-day event.

"I thought my brother might block for me today. Instead he totally kicked me under the bus as it roared by. He caught Bill's attention and volunteered me for the hero thing." The pure torment on Evan's face was almost comical. "I want to back out of it, but Bill played the 'it's for the kids' card, and now I think I'm trapped."

LIEXP0420

"Look, Mommy!" Sawyer ran over to them. A grubby, slimy—and very dead—worm rested in the palm of his hand.

"Ew."

At her disgust, Sawyer showed the prize to Evan. "Good find. He looks like he's dead, though, so you'd better give him a proper burial."

"Yeah!" Sawyer hurried over to the patch of dirt. He plopped the worm onto the sidewalk and told it to "stay" just like he would Belay. That made both of them laugh. Then he used one of the sticks as a shovel and began digging a hole.

"He's like a cat, always bringing me dead animals as gifts. I'm surprised he doesn't leave them for me on the doorstep."

Evan chuckled while waving toward the parking lot. She turned to see his brother and Mackenzie walking to their vehicle.

"Do you guys want to come out to Wilder Ranch for lunch? I'm sure they wouldn't mind two more. It's a happy sort of chaos there with all of the kids."

Addie's heart constricted at the offer. No doubt Sawyer would love it. She wanted exactly what Evan was offering, but all of that was off-limits for her. She couldn't allow herself any more access into Evan's world or vice versa.

"We can't, but thanks. I've got to get Sawyer down for a nap." Addie wasn't about to attempt attending a meeting with a tired Sawyer, and she didn't have anywhere else in town for him to go.

Evan's face morphed from relaxed to taut, but he didn't press further. "Right. Okay. I guess I'll see you later then." After saying goodbye to Sawyer, he caught up with Jace and Mackenzie in the parking lot.

A momentary flash of loss ached in Addie's chest. A few days in Evan's presence and he was already showing her how different things could have been. It was like there was a life out there that she'd missed by taking the wrong path. It was shiny and warm and so, so out of reach.

And the worst of it was, until Evan, she hadn't realized just how much she was missing.

Don't miss
Her Hidden Hope *by Jill Lynn,*
available May 2020 wherever
Love Inspired books and ebooks are sold.

LoveInspired.com

LIEXP0420